THE GOVERNESS CLUB: CLAIRE

By Ellie Macdonald

THE GOVERNESS CLUB: CLAIRE

ELLIE MACDONALD

AVONIMPULSE

An Imprint of HarperCollinsPublishers

Excerpt from *The Governess Club: Bonnie* copyright © 2013 by Heather Johnson.

Excerpt from *Skies of Gold* copyright © 2013 by Zoë Archer.

Excerpt from *Crave* copyright © 2013 by Karen Erickson.

Excerpt from *Can't Help Falling in Love* copyright © 2013 by Cheryl Harper.

Excerpt from *Things Good Girls Don't Do* copyright © 2013 by Codi Gary.

EPub Edition SEPTEMBER 2013 ISBN: 9780062292179

Print Edition ISBN: 9780062292216

JV 10 9 8 7 6 5 4 3 2 1

For my family. Thanks for your support and your speechlessness.

ACKNOWLEDGMENTS

Many thanks to everyone at the Avon Impulse team for bringing this all together, especially my editor, Tessa Woodward, for taking a chance on me and all of her patience; I wouldn't have done this without her. Also special thanks to Toby Anne for her willingness to help and obsess along with me. She was there every step of the way with a glass of wine in her hand and glitter in her hair.

PROLOGUE

"Can any of you honestly say she hasn't thought about it?"

Silence reigned; teacups hovered between saucer and mouth. Eyes flitted away with guilt —or secret shame, unwilling to admit that it had indeed crossed their minds.

"You're not being fair," one chided softly.

"But who genuinely wants this for the rest of their lives?"

"There's nothing wrong with being a governess," another chimed in.

"Of course not. Not if one disregards the fact that for women of our station it signifies a lowering of one's situation. We were not born to be in service."

"It's not quite service, per se . . ."

"How is it anything else? We are being paid to render a service. Our lives are theirs to dictate. I cannot even count the number of times I have been called upon to even out the numbers at a dinner party. And they think they are bestowing some great honor upon me when they know full well I have attended more illustrious tables than theirs."

"Now you're just being aggressive."

"And I dislike the being termed 'one whom another pays for a service,'" said another. "It makes me feel dirty, like a . . ."

"Say it dear. A *whore*. We are being paid for a service, which in essence is exactly what a whore is paid for."

"I believe my half day is nearly up. It is a long walk back, and the children will be expecting me back for their evening meal. I have no wish to be caught in the rain." A small redhead pulled on her gloves and left the room.

"Louisa, what is the matter with you? You know very well your logic is flawed. The whole of the working class are paid for services; it is only a minority who have a negative stigma attached to them, and that is based on the service they render, not simply the fact that they are getting paid."

Louisa sighed and sipped her tea. "I didn't mean to offend anyone."

Claire patted her arm. "We know. And Sara knows that, I'm sure."

Bonnie spoke up. "What caused this rant, Louisa? You are not usually so ferocious in your opinions."

Staring into her tea, Louisa said, "The Waldrons had a house party last week. One of my brother's friends was a guest."

"Oh dear."

"When he first saw me, he seemed genuinely delighted. And he was. I welcomed his compliments and platitudes because it reminded me of how my life had been before . . . well, before. But when his attentions became more marked and aggressive, I knew the truth. All he said was . . . he said . . . that surely I must expect this as part of my duties."

"Did you—I mean did he—"

"One thing I can thank my brother for is teaching me how to defend myself against unwanted male attention." A small smile accompanied Louisa's words. Twin sighs of relief escaped her two friends, and she raised her eyes to theirs, beseeching their understanding. "There must be more to life for us than this. We were raised to expect better."

"But how?" asked Bonnie. "None of us earn enough money to live independently for the duration of our lives, and our marriage prospects have dwindled more quickly than our social statuses."

"It's not like we have regular exposure to the kind of gentlemen who would elevate us back up anyway, even if they could," Claire joined in. "The gentlemen we work for are already married, and their friends see us as nothing more than sport, if they see us at all. We can no longer trust gentlemen of the titled class."

"But who says we need a man or marriage to escape our positions? And who says that *independent* means *isolated*?" Louisa asked.

"I don't think I quite follow," Bonnie said.

Louisa turned to Claire. "Have you made any progress on Ridgestone?"

Claire blinked. "No, but my father's—*my* solicitor remains optimistic."

"And each of us has been saving our wages, correct? Even Sara, I'm sure." At the confirming nods, Louisa became more adamant. "We could do it."

"Do what?"

"We could pool our resources and live independently, yet not isolated, and without marriage. Say we continue saving our money for three more years, five at most. That would give Claire ample time to see if regaining Ridgestone is possible and for us to save nest eggs capable of supporting us, albeit not in the style we were raised, but still comfortably. If Ridgestone is a possibility, then we already have a place to live. If not, then with all four of us contributing, we could afford a place large enough for the four of us."

"But houses cost money to maintain. How would we manage that if we no longer have our incomes?" Bonnie asked.

"We could still hire out our services as sort of tutors to young ladies and boys in want of preparation for school. Continue being teachers privately, not governesses, and maintain control over our own lives." Louisa beamed at her own ingenuity.

"You are sounding like Mary Wollstonecraft," Bonnie warned. "You've been reading her books and tracts again, haven't you?"

"What is wrong with thinking there is more to life? Why is it sinful for a woman to be treated equally and live independent of men?"

Claire and Bonnie exchanged a glance.

"I suppose that it is possible," Claire said.

"The idea does seem appealing," Bonnie agreed.

"I would much rather live with my three friends and be mistress of my own fate than have the Waldrons breathing down my neck," Louisa said emphatically.

Claire gave a wry smile. "That is certainly a ringing endorsement."

The others laughed. "Still, there is much to be thought upon and worked out," Bonnie cautioned. "Much can happen in five years."

"We have five years to do so," Louisa said.

"And Sara? Do you think she would be willing to join the club?" Claire asked.

"We have five years to convince her of that, too," Louisa answered. "And I like that idea—a club. Ladies and gentlemen have their exclusive clubs and gatherings that we cannot participate in; this is something that *they* cannot participate in. I say we make this entirely our own. Governesses only."

"A governess club?" Bonnie said with a smile.

"Indeed. And furthermore, we should have a motto," Louisa declared.

Claire laughed. "Like what?"

Louisa considered for a moment. "I know it is not an original idea, but perhaps 'All for one and one for all.'"

It was Bonnie's turn to laugh. "We are not defending the French monarchy, Louisa."

"No," she agreed solemnly. "We are fighting for our lives."

And thus, the Governess Club was born.

CHAPTER ONE

June 1822

"**M**iss Bannister! Miss Bannister!"

Six pairs of eyes looked up at the call; six pairs watched a maid hurry across the green lawn toward the trees. "Miss Bannister!" This time the maid added a wave, just to ensure she was noticed.

Miss Claire Bannister turned her pair of eyes back to her charges. "Keep sketching, children, while I speak with Lucy. Miss Allison, what a lovely shade of purple that hair is." The four-year-old beamed up at her as Claire stood and made her way toward the approaching servant.

"Miss," Lucy puffed as the two met, "there's a London gent in Mrs. Morrison's parlor fer ya."

"What?" Claire asked, surprised.

"A London gent. He said he was to meet with you, Mr. Fosters, and Mrs. Morrison. They're all there, waitin' fer ya."

Claire pressed a bewildered hand to her forehead. "What does he want?"

"I dunno, Miss, they didn't tell me. You'd best hurry; it took some time to find you, and they've been waitin' an age."

"Indeed." Glancing back at the group under the tree, Claire started toward the manor. "Please watch the children for me. I will return as soon as I am able."

"Yes, Miss," Lucy replied with a quick curtsey.

What would a "London gent" want with her, Claire wondered as she quickened her pace. The only man she knew in the capital was Mr. Baxter, her late father's solicitor. Why would he come all the way here instead of corresponding through a letter as usual? Unless it was something more urgent than could be committed to paper. Perhaps it had something to do with Ridgestone—

At that thought, Claire lifted her skirts and raced to the parlor. Five years had passed since her father's death, since she had to leave her childhood home, but she had not given up her goal to one day return to Ridgestone.

The formal gardens of Aldgate Hall vanished, replaced by the memory of her own garden; the terrace doors no longer opened to the ballroom, but to a small, intimate library; the bright corridor darkened to a comforting glow; Claire could even smell her old home as she rushed to the door of the housekeeper's parlor. Pausing briefly to catch her breath and smooth her hair, she knocked and pushed the door open, her head held high, barely able to contain her excitement.

Cup and saucer met in a loud rattle as a young man hurried to his feet; Mrs. Morrison's disapproving frown could not stop several large drops of tea from contaminating her white linen, nor could Mr. Fosters' harrumph. Claire's heart sank as she took in the man's youth, disheveled hair, and rumpled clothes; he was decidedly *not* Mr. Baxter. Perhaps a new associate? Her heart picked up slightly at that thought.

Claire dropped a shallow curtsey. "You wished to see me, Mrs. Morrison?"

The thin woman rose and drew in a breath that seemed to tighten her face even more with disapproval; she gestured to the stranger. "Yes. This is Mr. Jacob Knightly. Lord and Lady Aldgate have retained him as a tutor for the young masters."

Claire blinked. "A tutor? I was not informed they were seeking—"

"It is not your place to be informed," the butler, Mr. Fosters, cut in.

Claire immediately bowed her head and clasped her hands in front of her submissively. "My apologies. I overstepped." Her eyes slid shut and she took a deep breath to dispel the disappointment. Ridgestone faded into the back of her mind once more.

Mrs. Morrison continued with the introduction. "Mr. Knightly, this is Miss Bannister, the governess."

Mr. Knightly bowed. "Miss Bannister, it is a pleasure to make your acquaintance."

Claire automatically curtseyed. "The feeling is mutual, sir." As she straightened, she lifted her eyes to properly survey the new man. Likely not yet thirty, Mr. Knightly wore his brown hair long enough to not be following the current fashion. Scattered locks fell across his forehead, and a darkening of a beard softened an otherwise square-jawed face. Standing nearly a head taller than herself, his loosely fitted jacket and modest cravat did nothing to conceal broad shoulders. Skimming her gaze down his body, she noticed a shirt starting to yellow with age and a plain brown waistcoat struggling to hide the fact that its owner was less than financially secure;

even his trousers were slightly too short, revealing too much of his worn leather boots. All in all, Mr. Jacob Knightly appeared to be the epitome of a young scholar reduced to becoming a tutor.

Except for his mouth. And his eyes. Not that Claire had much experience meeting with tutors, but even she could tell that the spectacles enhanced rather than detracted from the pale blueness of his eyes. The lenses seemed to emphasize their round shape, emphasize the appreciative gleam in them before Mr. Knightly had a chance to hide it. Even when he did, the corners of his full mouth still remained turned up in a funny half-smile, all but oozing confidence and assurance, bordering on an arrogance one would not expect to find in a tutor.

Oh dear. Claire sighed inwardly. Not only was the man handsome, but clearly, he knew it. There was little worse, in her opinion, than a man overconfident in his attractiveness. And if he were as intelligent as he was handsome, well, the arrogance may be well deserved, but still difficult to tolerate.

"You will take Mr. Knightly upstairs and show him the tutor's room and the nursery," Mrs. Morrison was saying. "You know the nursery best, so inform him of the schedule and expectations of the household. Prepare to introduce him to the children. I am sure his lordship would want the masters' education to begin promptly."

"Of course. Mr. Knightly, if you follow me." Claire turned to leave the room, hearing Jacob step behind her. Turning toward the servants' stairs, she stopped briefly at the kitchen door. "Mrs. Potter, this is Mr. Knightly, the new tutor. He is moving in today."

The cook looked up but didn't stop chopping the vegetables. "Good afternoon, Mr. Knightly. Breakfast is at half six in the morning. You will lunch and take cooked tea with the children; Miss Bannister will inform you of their schedule."

"Yes, ma'am." The man sounded amused. Claire continued toward the servants' stairs as he followed her. "Where is the nursery?" Jacob's deep voice echoed in the stairwell.

"The second floor, above the family wing and below the servants' quarters," Claire replied. "Your room will be next to it."

"That sounds . . . typical."

Claire glanced back at him. "Do you have any luggage?" She glanced pointedly at his hands, empty except for a threadbare hat.

He stopped and blinked at her in confusion. "Wouldn't a footman—oh, right." He gave her a sheepish look. "Excuse me." Claire stood patiently when a few moments later Jacob returned, portmanteau in hand. He grinned. "Luggage retrieved."

She continued up the stairs. "There are five children, three girls and two boys, the twins. Masters Peter and Michael are only seven—"

"A good age to start their education," Mr. Knightly said.

Arrogant male. "Their education started when I arrived, Mr. Knightly," Claire said.

"Of course. And twins? Identical?"

"Yes. Not to worry, however. When they were born, Lord Aldgate cut a piece of Michael's—the younger one—right lobe off to assist in telling them apart; he wanted no chance of any sort of discrepancy or deceit later in life."

"That seems dramatic." Mr. Jacob's voice was beginning to sound strained, and his breaths were coming in heavier puffs.

Claire opened a door and entered the nursery. "Miss Sophie is eleven, Miss Mary is nine, and Miss Allison is four. The children sleep in the rooms across the corridor but take their meals and lessons in here." One of the doors on the far side swung open and a maid exited, her arms full with cleaning supplies. "This is Lucy, who is assigned to the nursery; she assists with meals and cleaning and supervision. This is your room." Claire indicated the door and stood off to the side, allowing him to enter.

Jacob lumbered past her, his face red from carrying his trunk. Placing it on the floor with a loud *thump*, he straightened with a groan. Catching her look, the groan cut off quickly, and he glanced around instead, turning his back to her as he rotated on the spot. Shock and disbelief began to show on his face.

"Is there something amiss with the room?" Claire asked.

"No, no, it's just—unexpected." Jacob moved over to the window and pushed the thin curtain aside. The view was merely a section of the roof covering a lower wing, just like hers on the other side of the wall. Inhaling deeply, he turned back toward her.

"Pray excuse me, Mr. Knightly. I must return to the children," Claire said. "We will be having cooked tea at half five; the children will be in bed by nine. We will be able to have further discussions then." She turned to leave.

"Jacob," he called out after her. "My name is Jacob."

Claire only paused to look over her shoulder. "Welcome to Aldgate Hall, *Mr. Knightly.*"

Jacob Knightly grinned as he watched the governess leave, her hips swaying nicely in her gray muslin dress. When the butler and housekeeper had told him to meet the governess, he had expected a short, plump, middle-aged dowd of a woman, the kind that haunts every young boy's dreams, not this brisk beauty he was presented with. True, she wasn't like the diamonds he was used to, but when she had burst into the housekeeper's parlor, face flushed and green eyes lit with anticipation, she had fairly radiated beauty.

His grin faded into a grimace as Jacob faced his room again. Gads, what a horrible excuse for sleeping quarters. If he spread out his arms, he was sure his fingers would touch both walls simultaneously. He tried it, just to be sure.

With a deep sigh, he flopped his arms back to his sides. At least the room was clean. Moving to the washstand, he splashed some cold water on his face to wash off the travel dust; sitting on the back of a horse cart was a dirtier mode of transport than he'd expected. Glancing into the small, warped mirror, he offered his reflection a cynical grin. If only his friends could see him now. None of them would believe that the Earl of Rimmel would voluntarily place himself in such circumstances. He barely believed it himself, but it seemed to be the best place for him, plain sight and all that; people saw what they wanted to see.

At that thought, he was reminded of his first slip-up, assuming that a footman would carry his luggage up the stairs. Jacob would have to get into the mindset of a servant if this was to have any hope of succeeding. Good thing Miss Bannister was there to bring his faux pas to his attention. The puerile part of his mind wondered what else she might instruct him on.

His thoughts back to her, Jacob threw himself onto the small bed and folded his hands behind his head. Squeaks rebounded off the wall with each movement, but he barely heard them, instead filling his head with the sight of a young, shapely governess. A speculative smile spread across his face once more as he contemplated turning every schoolboy's fantasy about prim, proper, pretty governesses into reality.

Well, he may be in voluntary exile for the time being, but no one said he couldn't have fun while he did it.

CHAPTER TWO

Claire winced as a loud creak wrenched through the silence. She quickly scanned the hall, her limbs ready to flee back up the stairs at the sight of the butler investigating the unexpected sound. Although Lady Aldgate had granted permission to the governess to make use of the library, Mr. Fosters had strict rules about staff wandering the manor house after hours.

Once she confirmed she had not been overheard, Claire silently chastised herself as she continued to make her way to the library. She knew the third step creaked but had not been paying attention. Instead, her mind had been on the new tutor. He had disappeared while she was putting the children to bed—the lack of light from under his chamber door led her to believe he had retired early—but not before making an impression on the female members of the staff during the afternoon. She, Mrs. Morrison, and Mrs. Potter seemed to be the only ones unaffected; every other body blessed with the female anatomy had been hanging on his every word, eating up his stories of London life like sweetmeats off a tray. Personally, Claire had found his general demeanor to be off-putting; arrogance and superiority seemed inherent to him, and she resented feeling as though she ought to be blessed to be sharing the table with him.

The library door opened on well-oiled hinges. Without hesitating, Claire moved toward the novels section, intent on finding a more interesting story than Defoe's disappointing sequel to *Robinson Crusoe*. Replacing said book back on the shelf, she ran her fingers over the spines, relishing the feel of them, clacking her fingers together.

Unable to settle on a novel, her fingers continued to dance over the spines, the indecision making her restless. She let her shawl fall back from her shoulders and she shifted her weight to one leg, her head cocking to the same side. A frustrated huff left her.

"Having difficulty finding something to read?"

The unexpected deep voice close behind her caused a small shriek to escape Claire. Whirling around with wide eyes, she pressed her back to the bookcase. The candlestick in her hand, wavering frantically in tune with her fright, cast a glow over Jacob's face where he stood a few feet away from her. Claire pressed a hand to her heart. "Goodness, you nearly scared the wits out of me."

Jacob chuckled. "A witless governess—that would be something to see."

Recovering slightly at his obvious humor, she frowned. "I do not appreciate being snuck upon, Mr. Knightly."

He continued to grin. "I wasn't skulking about. I was sitting in plain sight when you entered the room." His gesture indicated an overstuffed chair set back in one of the corners near a window.

Swallowing the last of her fright, Claire moved past him further into the room. "Fosters has strict rules about staff roaming the halls at night. He doesn't like it." A single candelabra lit the sitting area just enough for reading; Mr. Knightly must have been here for quite some time. "You should know that the common way of things is to take a book back to your quarters, not read it here.!" She spied a half-full tumbler of amber liquid. She whirled back around. "Are you drinking Lord Aldgate's Scotch?" She darted glances at the still open door.

Jacob shrugged and closed the door. "Again, I was told I could use the library freely." He moved to a chair that held an open book and picked it up.

"The books, not the furniture, and most certainly not the spirits. The generosity of the Aldgates only goes so far."

"Then they should have specified." The man was unconcerned as he waved his book in the air. "Have you read this one, *Tom Jones*? It's quite good."

"You're splitting hairs. Do you want to lose your position?"

"Why are you whispering?"

"I told you, Fosters has strict rules about staff being about at night." Claire shot another glance at the door, as though she could see through it.

Jacob bent his head conspiratorially in her direction. "I think we're safe," he whispered. "I'm pretty sure I heard the old man snoring when I walked past his room earlier. Besides," he straightened and resumed a normal speaking voice, "we'll just be careful not to get caught."

"Not getting caught does not mean a transgression has not been committed."

"Indeed not. But it does mean we will escape punishment." He picked up the tumbler and gave her a small salute with it before draining its contents.

"Have you no concern about what is at stake here? You could lose your position. I could lose my position merely by association."

"Then perhaps you should leave. Heaven forbid you be tainted by my actions." He turned his back on her.

Claire looked at his back through narrowed eyes. Good manners dictated she not say what was on her mind. The book clutched in her hands, she turned and marched out the door. As he said, best that she leave; she had too much at stake. The first good thing he had said since his arrival.

The next evening

Claire shut the door to the girls' room as softly as she could and rested her head against it, a weary sigh escaping her. After a rough day, Miss Allison had finally fallen asleep. A bee sting followed by a fall in the mud had caused the youngest girl to melt into a temper for the rest of the day, one that irked her sisters and brothers, further escalating the situation. And Mr. Knightly had been of no assistance; he hadn't even made an appearance before noon, and even when he had, he'd had no concept of how to talk to or relate to the children.

"Here now, Miss." Lucy was already in the nursery. "I've got the tea all set up. Even stole some of those sweet biscuits from Mrs. Potter. After the day you've had, you need 'em."

Claire's smile was tired, but grateful. "You are wonderful,." Lucy handed her a cup. Claire's eyes went up after taking a sip, and she started coughing. "Lucy, this is more than just tea!"

The maid grinned. "Like I said, you need it." The two giggled.

"So Fosters' rules about wandering the corridors frighten you, but you have no problem slipping a little tot into your tea?"

Claire stopped laughing and looked at Jacob standing in the entrance to his room. No coat or cravat, his waistcoat opened, a book in his hand. He grinned and sauntered over and sat in one of the chairs. "Don't stop on my account. Fix me one."

Lucy and Claire exchanged a glance, but the maid complied. Claire sipped her tea, her gaze unfocused on the tray on the table.

"I've always wondered what governesses and maids did once all the work was done. I'm looking forward to the exposé. My thanks, sweetheart." His gaze raked over Lucy before doing the same to Claire. "What comes next?"

Claire cleared her throat. "This is your first position in service?"

"Why? What makes you think that?"

"Do you need a list?"

He blinked. "Am I that obvious? And I thought governesses taught manners." Claire and Lucy exchanged another glance, one that Jacob did not miss. "I apologize. That was rude of me. Start at the top, then."

"Excuse me?"

"Why is it so obvious this is my first position?"

The ladies shared a third glance. "Will you stop doing

that? I feel like you're having a telepathic conversation about me."

Lucy leaned toward to Claire. "What's tela—tello—"

"Telepathic," Claire supplied quietly. "Greek for talking with one's mind."

"Blimey, people kin do that? Well then, maybes we is havin' a tellopraptic conversation," Lucy said. She smiled at Claire over her teacup.

Claire placed her empty teacup on the table and took control of the conversation. "You've been here for a week, and you've yet to demonstrate any subservient behavior."

"What do you mean?"

"You enter a room as though you own it and expect everyone to do your bidding."

"I do not."

"How did you get that cup of tea? Were you invited to join us?"

Jacob looked at her for a moment, rubbing under his nose with a finger. "Point taken." "Second, you get out of sorts when you have to do things for yourself."

"Examples?"

"Your first morning, you slept in and missed breakfast. You were annoyed at Lucy, all the lower servants, and myself for not waking you. You had to put your own laundry into the hamper three days ago; we heard about it in the nursery for the rest of the day. That night in the library—" Claire broke off. She hadn't told anyone of his appropriation of the scotch. "You barely show proper submissiveness to Fosters and Mrs. Morrison."

Mr. Knightly shrugged. "Perhaps I believe the class system is outdated. Equality is the way of the future."

A fourth glance shared, and a laugh this time. "You don't believe in equality," Claire said.

He turned to the maid. "Don't you speak at all?"

Lucy pulled back. "Ye like hearin' the same thing over? My words ain't as fancy as hers be, but they still got the same meanin'."

"Is this a conspiracy?" Jacob slumped back in his chair.

Claire pursed her lips in an attempt to keep from laughing. "Not particularly. It's not hard to see, even if one is not looking for it. Even now, what you just did, speaks to a life of getting what you want. You're not used to being thwarted, are you?"

He barely glanced at her.

"Why did you even become a tutor? It clearly does not suit you."

"According to you, nothing will suit me. I am not subservient enough."

"You do realize that you sound like the twins right now?"

Lucy stood and picked up the tray. "I'm thinkin' it be best for me to take this away. I know when to leave somethin' be." She gave Claire a significant look. She left the two sitting in silence, watching her leave.

The silence grew. Jacob was still sulking, and Claire had no wish to deal with another childish tantrum. Refusing to be pulled into his antics, she smoothed her skirts and stood. "Good night, Mr. Knightly." Her brisk steps took her to her door.

"Wait." His voice called out and stopped her before she could close the door.

"Mr. Knightly, I'm not really in the mood—"

"Look," he interrupted. He stood and ran a hand through his hair. "I don't have a choice. I need this tutor position, but as you so eloquently have put it, I am failing."

"I haven't even touched on your tutoring abilities yet."

His eyes shot a glare at her. "There is no need to be caustic."

"Yet so tempting." Claire couldn't hold back a small smirk. "It is clear that humility does not come naturally to you."

"At least I am trying."

Claire sobered herself at his petulant tone. He *was* trying, and that deserved some acknowledgement. She waited for him to speak again.

Jacob ran both hands through his hair, ferociously scratching the back of his head. He began to pace. His behavior took Claire by surprise; she had never seen a man so out of sorts before.

"See here," he finally said. "You must help me."

"I must?" Raised eyebrows accompanied her question.

"Yes. As I said, I need this position. Sparing you the details, I cannot return to London at this time."

"I see. Yet I fail to see the part where I *must* help you."

"I thought I made it clear. You will give me advice on how to navigate the world of servitude."

Claire folded her arms and let out a long sigh. "It is like dealing with a seven-year-old."

"Excuse me?"

"This piece of advice is free of charge and given with no obligation or expectation of more to be given. Understood?"

Jacob nodded and gestured magnanimously.

"Servants are ordered around enough by their employers; even within their ranks, the upper servants have the authority and power, and order the lowers around. As used as they are to feeling insignificant and debased, they are human and prefer to be treated as such."

Jacob was confused. "I don't follow."

"Ask, Mr. Knightly, don't demand. Especially of servants who occupy the same sphere of relevance as you. So before I offer you any more advice on how to 'navigate the world of servitude,' I would appreciate if you ask for my help, not demand and expect me to comply."

"I didn't—"

"Try to not embarrass yourself again by having me point out your mistakes. I truly dislike that game; no one enjoys having their flaws pointed out, even if they asked to hear them."

"Gads, you really have the governess role down to a tee. Do you ever relax and stop disciplining people? It makes one feel judged—and found lacking."

Claire took a deep breath. He was right. She should not be treating him so. "My apologies. I did not mean to be so insulting."

A wry grin tugged at the corners of him mouth. "I often tend to bring out the worst in people."

"But that does not excuse my behavior. And despite the frequency, I suspect that one would not appreciate such a characterization. I will endeavor to not add to it."

It was his turn to look at her silently. For the space of several heartbeats, all he did was stare at her, those pale blue eyes filled with disbelief and surprise. For the first time since his arrival, the effect of those eyes spread over her. So different from the studied gleam usually found in them, this odd unexpected vulnerability sang of sincerity, drawing her in and settling in her chest.

It took several moments and a deep, awkward clearing of his throat, but Jacob finally spoke. "Thank you. I appreciate your efforts."

Jacob could not remember feeling so out of sorts. The disdain, the dismissal from others—he was used to that; no one ever took him seriously. But this? This outright admission that her treatment of him had been wrong? Despite it being so similar to what he had heard his entire life? What did that mean?

He fell back on the behavior that had been engrained in him as a noble gentleman since birth. Giving her a shallow bow, he gestured to the chair she had been sitting in. "Shall we have a seat and discuss our project?"

She smoothed her skirts and stood a bit straighter; if she was suspicious of his sudden solicitousness, she didn't give any indication. With a nod, she crossed over to the table and perched on the edge of the chair, folding her hands on her lap. It was a gesture he had seen in countless ladies in the same position; it suddenly became clear where each of them had learned it from. The sudden obviousness made him feel stupid, but Jacob stamped that down and sat down across from her.

"Miss Bannister, I find I am struggling with the new circumstances in which I find myself. I would greatly appreciate any assistance you could provide."

She nodded again. "I would be happy to help where I can."

"My thanks." Jacob resisted the urge to replicate her nod. "As you have noted, I am unused to a life of servitude. While

I have not had the most privileged life"—the lie stuck in his throat for a moment—"I have never needed to do for others or serve them. I do not know how to behave in this situation."

Claire looked down at her hands. "It is not easy to debase oneself."

That comment caught his attention. "How did you find yourself being a governess?"

She didn't answer right away. When she did, her voice was quiet but confident. "I was a companion first. For nearly a year. But . . . some things happened, and I had to find a new position. Lady Aldgate was my second interview through the London agency. She liked me, and here I am. That was four years ago."

That wasn't quite the answer he was looking for. "And why did you become a companion? This couldn't have been your lifelong dream."

A hard look from her. "My next piece of advice: don't belittle the choices of others. This one is universal, not just limited to how to survive as a servant. You have no concept of what their dreams or ambitions are."

He sighed. "I have only known you for a week, but I have apologized more to you than I have to anyone in my entire lifetime."

"Perhaps that could be an indication that your behavior needs to be changed."

"Was being a companion or a governess your ambition?"

"There is nothing wrong with either position."

Jacob thought she sounded too defensive. "But were they what you wanted from life?"

She was silent for several beats. "No," she finally admitted.

Jacob waited for her to say more. "That's it? That's all you're going to say?"

"I thought we were supposed to be talking about you."

He grunted. "I'm not going to fall for that trap. If I agree with you, I sound like a conceited ass, but if I disagree with you, I end up being annoyingly persistent. Either way I lose."

Claire sighed. "I don't understand why we constantly rub each other the wrong way. I am not usually so argumentative."

Jacob had his theories about that. He hadn't stopped thinking about her since the moment they met, and his resolution to seduce her hadn't disappeared. It was frustrating that this was the first time he had been able to talk to her alone. All week he had watched her, growing more and more fascinated each time she smiled and laughed with the children or the maid Lucy. At meals, he could hardly keep his gaze off her dignified posture; he had never considered cheekbones to be an attractive feature, but hers, gently arched, gave her an endearingly noble air, lending the impression of some Roman empress gracing her subjects with her presence. Her warm smile reduced any possible sense of haughtiness and distance, though, drawing in those to whom it was directed. God, he ached to have that smile turned toward him.

That, combined with this conversation, set a niggling thought in the back of his mind that Claire Bannister was more than a woman to be seduced. Thankfully, he was adept at ignoring such righteous thoughts.

CHAPTER THREE

Jacob stared in frustration at the blank faces staring back at him. Even after several attempts, the boys still did not understand the concept. "Look, potential energy is when an object is not in motion; the energy is stored within it. When that energy is released, either through internal or external means, and thus begins to move, that energy shifts from being potential to actual, known as *kinetic*, energy."

"I'm hungry. When's lunch?" Michael asked.

"I have to wee really bad," Peter offered.

"I'll help you wee!" Michael shouted and tackled his brother, tickling him. The two bodies tangled together and rolled all across the floor.

"No, no, stop. Don't tickle me. You're going to make me wee. Stop, don't do that!" Peter's giggling voice reverberated through the small schoolroom, Michael's adding to the volume.

"That is enough!" Jacob roared, pulling the two boys apart. "You are not paying attention. Behavior like this will only get you caned, and trust me, I can wield a cane better than you have ever seen in your short lives so far. Now what?" he spit out as he looked at the boys' red faces.

Michael pointed at Peter. "He wee'd on me."

Jacob looked down at the boys' legs, and sure enough, both sets were sporting wet spots. With a growl, he yanked open the door to the nursery. "Miss Bannister, if you please." The bustle of skirts precipitated her arrival at the door and Jacob pointed at the boys. "Take care of that . . . incident."

Her eyes wide, Claire took in the scene as the boys looked on, abashed. Once she had properly assessed the situation, her lips pursed together, a stern, disappointed look was given to the boys, and she pointed toward their room. "Really, boys. At seven years of age, this is what happens? How disgusting." Quiet apologies to her and himself were muttered as the boys sulked out of the room.

Jacob strode to the window and threw it open, releasing the stench of the incident from the room. Closing his eyes, he leaned against the windowpane, dragging in deep breaths of the fresh air. Good Lord, what had he gotten himself into? He had had no idea being a tutor was so frustrating. Had he been like that as a pupil? He could only assume so. All Jacob could remember was the desperate desire to be outside instead of shackled to the schoolroom. He lifted his eyes to the spotless blue sky, taking in the sun reflecting off the small pond and the trees swaying in the cooling breeze. A day like today would have been torture for him as a pupil; so many other things beckoned. Perhaps he should just let the brats run loose; it wasn't as though he was a real tutor, by any stretch of the imagination. He didn't even anticipate being here much longer than a month anyway.

A vision of Miss Bannister's face came to mind, lips pursed and eyes glinting with that strange combination of sternness and disappointment that only governesses and mothers could achieve. He could even hear her voice, that practical tone of hers: *The most important thing I feel I can teach them is to not give up, that through determination and effort they can achieve their goals.*

With a snort, Jacob pushed himself away from the windowpane. Giving up. The one thing he did well in life, according to his father. Had anyone taught him the way Miss Bannister taught her charges? No one came to mind.

Think like a child. Miss Bannister's advice from last night rang in his head. *Just try to remember what you would have enjoyed. Not much has changed in twenty years; quite possibly the children will like it as well. Even if they don't, you have learned something about them.*

Jacob's eyes focused on the trees again. A foreign feeling came over him, one that made him think that perhaps this would be one time that he wouldn't fail. Striding to the door, he called out, "Gentlemen, we are going tree climbing."

Jacob positioned the brothers at the base of the tree, poised to climb. "Right now, you are still, not in motion. But that does not mean that nothing is happening. Right now, you are full of potential energy. Do you know what *potential* means?"

"It's like a promise," Peter chirped.

"That's right. Right now you are full of the promise of energy, the promise of movement. Scientifically, it is referred to as potential energy. Once you start moving, however, it changes from potential energy to kinetic energy. Can you guess what *kinetic* means?"

"Is it like *kindle*, to start a wood fire?" Peter asked.

"Or like kite flying?" Michael offered.

"If potential energy means the promise of moving, but it keeps that promise by changing to kinetic energy, what do you think might have happened?"

"Did it start moving?"

"Exactly! Kinetic energy means that something has started to move. Now, as I said, right now you two are full of potential energy. I want you to get to the first branch by changing your potential energy into kinetic energy."

"You mean you want us to climb the tree?" Peter asked. Michael had already started scrambling up the trunk. Within minutes, both boys were sitting on the first branch, slightly above Jacob's head.

"Well done, gentlemen. Remind me, what does it mean when something has potential energy?"

"It isn't moving."

"And what does it mean when something has kinetic energy?"

"It is moving, like climbing a tree."

"Excellent." Much better. Jacob felt a surge of something in his chest, expanding and warming him all over. "Those two things are energies. Let's talk about a particular force right now." Helping the boys move, he quickly had them hanging from the branch by their hands. "How does it feel to be hanging there?"

"The bark is hurting my hands," Michael complained.

"It will do that. Later we'll talk about why trees are made

the way they are. Right now, try pulling yourselves up." The boys struggled and managed to move themselves somewhat, but essentially remained in the same position.

"Mr. Knightly, my arms are hurting," Peter whined.

"Why do they hurt? Why don't you pull yourself up onto the branch?"

"I'm trying, but it's hard. There's something pulling me down!"

"Exactly. That's the force we're going to talk about." Gently he lifted each boy down and they all sat on the grass, the boys rubbing their arms. "Both of you felt something pulling you down when you were hanging. That is a force called *gravity*. It's something invisible from the earth that pulls things down to the ground. You see the leaves and branches on the tree? Most of them are pointing toward the ground. That is because gravity has a good grip on them and is pulling them back down."

"Does the earth have invisible arms?" Michael asked.

Jacob chuckled. "I guess you could say that. Gravity is like the earth reaching out and grabbing hold of something, pulling it back to the ground. The bigger something is, the better grip gravity can have on it, making it more difficult for something to move away from the earth."

"Is that why birds fly and we don't?" Michael asked. "Because we're bigger than them?"

"Partly. We can talk more about the differences between human and bird anatomy later." He glanced up and spotted their sisters and governess heading their way with a picnic basket. "Why don't you give Miss Bannister a demonstration of your kinetic energy?"

With eager cries, the boys streaked off toward the approaching group, hollering at the top of their lungs about their kinetic energy. Even from that distance, Jacob could feel Claire's gaze on him.

He just smiled.

Jacob rose from his chair as Claire entered the room with a freshly washed Miss Allison, the other two girls following behind. Noticing the boys still in their seats, he cleared his throat and got their attention. "Stand up, gentlemen."

The twins obeyed, starting to scramble toward the table, where Lucy was setting up cooked tea. Jacob managed to grab both boys by their collars and held them firmly, making the struggles futile.

"Let me go!" Peter demanded, but Jacob simply watched the girls and Claire take their places. Once they were settled, Jacob shook the boys slightly. "What was that for?" Michael asked, disgruntled. "You said to stand, so we did. Why did you grab us?"

"You were not standing in order to go to the table," Jacob said in a calm but firm voice. "Ladies had entered the room. Gentlemen do not sit so long as ladies have entered the room and not yet taken a seat."

The twins were bewildered. "Ladies? Where?" Jacob nodded his head in the direction of the table. "They're not ladies," Peter scoffed. "They're girls!"

Jacob moved toward the table and took his seat at the head of it, opposite Claire at the foot. The boys followed. "They are ladies because they are the daughters of a lord, just as being the sons of a lord makes you gentlemen."

"Ladies do not stick out their tongues, Miss Mary," Claire admonished. Lucy began serving the plates as Claire poured the weak tea.

"But they said we were girls," she protested.

"Did they lie? Are you not a girl?"

"But—"

"No buts. If you want your brothers to see you as a lady, you must act as one."

"The same goes for you," Jacob told the twins. "There is more to being a gentleman than to whom you were born. It is a behavior that you learn; it is how you treat others. One of those behaviors is to show respect to ladies by standing when they enter a room and not sitting until they do."

"I don't understand why that shows respect," Peter grumbled. He glared at his sweet bun, tearing small bits off it.

"Nevertheless, it is something you must do if you want people to respect you." Jacob said. He caught Claire's eye and held it as he added, "Besides, there are more ladies in the room than you realize."

Claire's eyes widened in surprise at his comment and a slight flush covered her cheeks. Jacob's eyes were drawn to that small bit of color, basking in the effect of his compliment. Had no one ever called her that?

"Excuse me," Claire said, rising from the table. "I will see if Lucy needs any help." Her voice lacked her usual confident briskness, another sign that Jacob's comment had unsettled her. She left the room in a quick rustle of skirts.

"Do we have to stand every time *they* do as well?" Peter's moan brought attention to how Jacob had stood. The twins gave long-suffering sighs but followed suit.

"What do the girls do for us?" Michael demanded. "They get all the good stuff. I saw Papa give Mama a set of pearls, and all she did was *kiss* him." A dramatic shudder accompanied his comment.

"That's what girls are supposed to do," Mary chimed in. "That's where babies come from." She said this with an air of superior knowledge.

"Eww, that's disgusting," Peter said.

"I'm never kissing a girl," Michael concurred. "It's gross, pressing your lips against a girl. Papa and Mama even used their tongues. It makes me sick."

"Are we going to have another brother or sister?" Mary asked Jacob. He looked at her with panic in his throat, unsure of how to answer or to steer the conversation another direction.

Sophie rolled her eyes. "Kissing doesn't cause babies."

"I a stork!" Allison cried, putting her napkin in her mouth and flapping her arms. "See, I bringing a baby."

"Yes it does," Mary insisted. "Elizabeth Pike told me at church. That's why only husbands and wives kiss."

"Elizabeth Pike can barely put her hair up in the same ribbons. Babies come when husbands and wives kiss, hold hands, and be in a room alone together."

Allison slid off her chair and began her stork flight around the table, adding squawking to the performance. "I'm not standing for her," Peter said. "She may be a girl, but she's just a baby, not a lady." He frowned mulishly and shoved a large bit of biscuit in his mouth, crumbs falling around him.

"Elizabeth has four older sisters, one who is married. She knows all about how babies are made, and you don't." Mary glared at Allison.

"They were going like this." Michael demonstrated the art of kissing, making it a dreadful experience.

Jacob's head spun with how quickly the cooked tea had spiraled out of control. He doubted Claire had even walked three steps from the nursery before all hell had broken loose. He was half tempted to run after her for assistance but didn't trust the little hoodlums to leave the nursery intact.

He got their attention by slamming his fist against the table. Plates and dishes rattled; tea spilled and stained the already stained tablecloth.

"That is enough." His voice was low and tight.

"You shouldn't hit the table like that," Sophie said.

"It might break," Michael continued.

"It would be a big mess," Peter joined in.

"And then where would we be?" Mary asked in a reasonable tone.

"Dead," was Allison's contribution from under the table. "Dead is bad."

A slow inhalation through his nose, released just as long, just as noisily. "This is what is going to happen . . ."

Claire could not believe her eyes. Upon returning to the nursery, she found its occupants—both child and adult—sitting around the table in absolute silence. The meal was still being consumed, eyes were moving to others suspiciously, lips were pressed shut and quivering to keep silent. The males of the room had risen, albeit reluctantly on the part of the younger two, but had not spoken.

Unsure of what was happening, Claire took her seat, her eyes on each of the children. No one spoke. Allison smiled and opened her mouth, but remembrance dawned on her face and she quickly snapped her mouth shut.

Claire looked across the table at Jacob. "What—"

"She spoke!" Peter crowed. "Miss Bannister spoke! She loses!" The other children chimed in, shattering the silence.

"Lost what?" Claire looked back at Jacob in confusion.

"We were playing the quiet game," Sophie explained over her brothers.

"The first person to speak loses," Mary added.

"And you spoke. You lost, you lost, you lost," Peter and Michael sang.

Allison's face began to crumple. "I don't want Miss Bannister to lose." Tears threatened her eyes.

"Ahem." Jacob's clearing throat and firm eyes quieted the noise. He gave his attention to Claire. "As the girls explained, the first person to speak in the quiet game loses. However," he cut off Peter's attempt to resume his chant, "as you were not in the room when it began and therefore did not know what we were playing, you did not technically lose."

"What?" protested Peter.

"How can someone lose a game they are not playing?" Jacob asked reasonably.

Slumping in his chair, Peter mumbled, "I suppose so."

"That means Peter spoke first," Sophie declared. "He is the loser!"

Peter's adamant returned immediately. "I am not!"

"Peter's the loser. Peter's the loser," the two elder girls chanted.

"Ladies, that is enough." Claire's clear voice rang over theirs, silencing the chant.

"I am not the loser," Peter said, glaring at his sisters.

"A gentleman accepts his losses with grace and pays his debts with honor," Jacob informed him.

"Being a gentleman is horrible."

Jacob ignored that. "But considering the circumstances, as supreme judge I declare the penalty null and void."

Claire addressed Sophie and Mary. "And ladies, poor losers are never respected, but poor winners are abhorrent."

"What's abhorrent?" Sophie asked.

"Extremely hateful," Claire supplied. "Such behavior calls for an apology." The girls muttered their apologies. "Now, I believe we are all finished here. Up and to your rooms. It's been a long day, so quiet time before bed is called for."

Despite their protests, the children were herded into their respective rooms. Jacob sat back in his chair and watched the sway of Claire's bottom as she brought up the rear of the line.

She looked over her shoulder before leaving the room. "What was the penalty for losing?"

He grinned. "Giving my sweaty, stinky feet a foot rub before going to bed."

Her laughter filled the room and lingered after she left, putting a smile on Jacob's face.

Chapter Four

Yet another surprise awaited Claire after the children had been put down, Mr. Knightly was crouching in front of the fire, stirring the embers. Cushions had been piled up around the hearth, and Claire noticed a tray bearing bread, cheese, ham, and sweetmeats nearby along with a decanter of wine and two glasses. A familiar toasting fork was propped up against the fireplace.

Hearing her enter, Jacob turned and stood, the fire poker hanging from his hand. He made a bow worthy of a courtier. "Good evening, Miss Bannister."

God in heaven, he was a beautiful man. Especially reflected in the firelight. Some candles remained lit, but the glow from the fireplace provided most of the illumination. Standing as he was, his features were covered in orange light, the shadows making his aristocratic features more prominent, more beautiful. Claire knew that *beautiful* was not a word usually associated with the males of the species, but nothing seemed more appropriate at the moment. The one regret was that the reflection of light on his spectacles distorted her view of his gentle blue eyes.

She cleared her throat. "What is all this?"

He smiled. "You did not eat much at dinner. I thought you might still be hungry."

His smile eased away some of her initial wariness, and Claire moved toward the setup. "How did you manage to get the tray?" she asked, settling down on the cushions. "Cook doesn't like preparing anything extra after the children have eaten. Even the tea tray is not a guarantee."

"Cook might not appreciate the extra work, but the undercook—now she's a different matter."

Claire sniffed. "All you have to do is smile at a lady and she does your bidding."

Jacob grinned. "It has worked so far."

"I give you fair warning, sir, that it will not work with me."

"But it already has." At her questioning look, he elaborated. "You're sitting on the cushions, are you not?"

Claire pursed her lips in response, but could not maintain the righteous indignation. Her lips eased and she shared a tentatively amused smile with him.

"There it is," Jacob said softly. His heart beat a bit harder at the sight of her smile. "You really shouldn't scrimp on your smiles. They have the power to make men do foolish things."

Heat flooded Claire's cheeks; she was sure her face was bright red and knew that it wasn't from sitting too close to the fire. "Foolish things like what?" she asked.

"Fishing for compliments?" he teased. "It can make a man requisition a tray for toasties and spread cushions on the floor just for the promise of seeing that smile."

"I never asked—"

"I know."

Claire couldn't seem to break away from his gaze. The dratted firelight still prevented a clear view of his eyes, but she could feel their power settling over her. "Do you need your spectacles?" she blurted without thought. "I beg your pardon. Of course you need them; you wear them all the time."

"Actually, I don't need them." Jacob slid them off his face and folded them up, sliding them into his shirt pocket. "They're made of glass. I wear them so others will take me seriously as a tutor. They are merely a prop for the image I wish to convey."

The clear, unhindered view of his eyes stole Claire's breath away. When she had first seen them upon his arrival, the pale blueness had brought to mind ice. But now, experiencing the smile imbedded in them, the appreciation—how could *ice* be so warm? No, the color now reminded her of a robin's egg, and just as that egg holds the promise of new life, his eyes also held a promise. But of what?

Regaining control of her wits, Claire focused on what he had said. "Why do you feel compelled to give the image of a tutor? You are one; there is no need to project a false idea of who you are."

Jacob remained silent, unable to speak. Another mistake. And given how perceptive this young governess was, he could not afford another one, lest his ruse be discovered.

Claire held out her hand and broke the moment. "Pass me the toasting fork."

Jacob grabbed it but refused to relinquish it. "Oh no, this is my treat for you. I am doing the work."

"It is hardly work to hold a piece of bread over embers."

"Ah, but when I make toasties, there is more to it than that. It is a veritable art form."

Claire smirked. "An art form?"

Jacob took a piece of bread and a knife. "Oh yes. I assure you my toasties were famous in my school halls. Many a young boy and chap would come, begging for a late-night nibble. Once, I even hosted my tutor for an evening meal."

Claire laughed, the image of a younger Jacob Knightly serving his tutor a cheese toastie. "Did he enjoy it?"

Jacob shot her a look, letting her how ridiculous he thought her question. "Of course. But the point of the toastie was not to impress him, but rather distract him from discovering I had yet again not completed my work." He began buttering one side of the bread before slipping it onto the toasting fork. Claire watched his hands as they gently clasped the handle, cradling the metal device in his fingers. She wondered how it would feel to have those fingers cradle her cheek at this moment—would they be cool from the metal or warm from the fire? She cleared her throat.

"And did that work?"

"No." A sheepish smile accompanied his answer, eliciting a giggle from her.

"I think you likely received your just desserts for that."

Jacob looked at her with mock severity. "Don't be so quick to judge, my dear. I highly doubt you were the model pupil to your own governesses."

"You think I had more than one?" The heat of the fire must be relaxing her. Claire's wariness had all melted away, and she began to recline on the piled cushions.

"Doesn't every girl go through more than one governess?"

"What makes you think I even had a one?"

"For starters," Jacob pulled the piece of toast from the embers and repeated the process with another piece of bread, "you are educated. That came from somewhere."

"It could have been my mother or a school," Claire argued.

Jacob stopped what he was doing and looked her directly in the eye. "Was it?"

The straightforwardness of his gaze and his question pierced through to the inside of her chest. He was dangerous when being sincere. Claire much preferred him this way to his arrogant demeanor, but knew it would behoove her to remember to tread carefully.

She sat up. "No. You were correct, but I only had one governess."

"A model pupil then." Jacob pulled the second piece of toast out. Claire watched as he placed a slice of cheese on either piece of toast and a thin wafer of ham on before folding them together to make a sandwich. Expecting him to hand it to her, she was surprised when he maneuvered the sandwich back onto the toasting fork and returned it to the heat.

"Perhaps not so model, but a patient governess," Claire said.

"So what happened?" Jacob had been waiting to try again at uncovering her past.

"What do you mean?"

"Your parents were well off enough to afford a governess for their daughter. Why did you have to become one yourself?"

"I am not comfortable with the direction of this conversation," Claire said. "It doesn't seem an appropriate time."

Jacob pulled the sandwich out of the fire and placed it on a plate before handing it to her. "Careful, it's hot. Give it a few moments to cool." He watched as Claire lifted the plate and puckered her lips, slowly blowing air onto the sandwich to cool it. The sight of her lips, rounded as for a kiss, sent his pulse racing.

She took a bite. "Oh, it's hot!"

"I warned you." He poured her a glass of wine.

She gave him an impish smile and accepted the offered glass. "I struggle with patience, especially when there is a treat involved. But you were telling the truth; this toastie is delicious. Much better than I have ever made."

He began to prepare another one. "That should teach you to doubt my word."

"In my defense, you did not precisely act trustworthy when you first arrived."

Claire saw his entire body still. Tension rippled through the air. "Whatever do you mean?" He tried for a nonchalant tone.

"May I be honest?"

"By all means."

Claire took another bite of her toastie, savoring the taste of the warmed cheese and ham on her tongue. "Your initial arrogance was very off-putting. It did not endear you in any way."

"My initial arrogance? Does that mean your impression has changed?" He sat back with his toastie and faced her.

Claire smiled. "You have made some improvement; your company has become more tolerable."

"Your flattery knows no bounds," Jacob replied wryly. He enjoyed seeing that twinkle in her eyes.

Claire laughed, a husky chuckle that went straight to his groin. Images of hearing that chuckle in his bed with her naked form twined around him flooded his brain. Sweet Mary, but it was warm in this nursery.

"Despite these improvements, however, you still feel you cannot confide in me," Jacob turned the conversation to less physically straining topics. " What better time to share a burden? It is merely you and I and the fire." He saw her hesitate again, glancing down at her half-eaten sandwich. "I admit to some selfishness here, Claire. You intrigue me; I wish to know more about you. More importantly, I want you to trust me."

Claire looked up at him, her eyes clouded with uncertainty. It struck Jacob that he had been very mistaken about her eyes. They weren't a mossy green, but rather grassy, emeraldy, a combination of all three. The different shades played together harmoniously, each allowing the others moments to shine. When she laughed, the emeralds twinkled with delight; when angered, the grass snapped; when content, the moss softened. This look, this confused uncertainty, blended all three into a shade he had never seen before, yet the impact thudded in his gut and echoed throughout his veins. At this moment in time, he would do whatever it took to banish that look from her eyes forever but had no idea how to accomplish it. God help him, he never wanted her to feel this again. *He* never wanted to feel this again.

Having never felt a symbiotic emotional experience, Jacob was shaken. Shoving the rest of the toastie in his mouth, he wiped his hands and poured himself some wine to wash it down. He needed some distance. "But you can keep your secrets if you wish. It makes no difference to me," he said around a mouthful of toastie. The wine quickly disappeared from his cup and he poured himself another.

He made the mistake of glancing at Claire. Her gaze distant, her face was turned toward the fire. The light caught her dark hair, sending slivers of gold swimming through her loosened coif. Some strands had escaped and fallen along her cheek, her soft cheek being caressed by the warm firelight.

Before he even knew what he was doing, Jacob had reached out and tucked the strands behind her ear. When she turned to look at him, it was natural to cup her cheek. Sweet Mary, but her cheekbones were magnificent.

Claire's breath hitched and her eyes slid shut as his thumb traced her cheekbone. She was not ignorant of relations between men and women, but it had been so long since a man had touched her; being constantly surrounded by children tended to daunt even the bravest of men. She hadn't even realized how much she missed having a beau's attention.

Feeling the cushions around her shift, Claire half opened her eyes to see Jacob moving toward her. His face intent, his eyes focused on her, his arm slid around her shoulders, and he gently lifted her chin with two fingers. Studying her face up close for a moment, he lowered his mouth toward her.

Claire could not mistake his intentions. Dear Lord, was this happening? Did she *want* this to happen? With Mr. Knightly? She could not deny that he was handsome, and she had not lied earlier when she said his company had improved upon her, but did she esteem him to the extent of wanting to encourage a deeper relationship with him?

Her moment of indecision nearly took the choice away

from her. At the last moment, she turned her head, and his lips met her cheek rather than her mouth. Sensations swirled at the touch of his strong, warm lips against her skin, spiraling all the way down to her belly. Her eyes slid shut again when he continued to press little kisses, following her cheekbone in the direction of her ear. She instinctively tilted her head to give him better access.

Instead of capturing her ear, Jacob surprised her by going for her chin. "You have some cheese here," he murmured, licking it off before pressing his lips to the same spot. "Mmm, cheddar has never tasted so good."

Horrified, Claire pulled away and fumbled for a napkin, handkerchief, anything to wipe her face. How embarrassing to be caught with food on her face!

But Jacob merely pulled her back into his embrace, raising his own handkerchief to wipe the offending spot. He smiled. "Better?"

Claire was sure her face was fifty shades of scarlet. She could barely speak, the conflicting emotions of pleasurable tension and embarrassment closing her throat. Jacob tightened his arm around her shoulders and rubbed her arm, staring into the fire.

Slowly, Claire began to relax and became aware of all the surrounding sensations. Pressed against his side, she became aware of a physical strength his loose clothing hid; the arm around her was heavy with muscle, but comfortingly so, not intimidating in any sense. A mixture of bay rum and wine fused together and wafted around her, giving him a unique scent that raised the little hairs on her arm. Claire felt the sudden urge to press her nose to his neck and inhale deeply.

Instead, she focused on the heat shifting from his body to hers, threatening her muscles with languid contentment.

She could not stop the sigh escaping from her nor the shift in her body, pressing her deeper into his embrace, lulled by his heat and the steady stroking of her upper arm. Good heavens, but this was nice.

Jacob did not attempt to break the silence; it was Claire who spoke first.

"I was betrothed, once."

The stroking paused for a moment, the only indication that he heard her; Jacob remained silent.

"His name was Thomas, and he served as a footman to the lady who employed me as a companion. She was old and frail, but kindhearted. As first positions go, I was incredibly fortunate and enjoyed working for her.

"Thomas was smart and ambitious; he intended to work his way up to butler. Of course he knew that it was unlikely in Lady Allen's household. No one expected her to live much longer than two more years. But still, he had dreams."

The arm stroking stopped, but Jacob didn't release her. "What happened?"

"I never expected to find romance, but he made me laugh. The first time he did, it felt like I hadn't laughed in years. And I hadn't. My mother died when I was fifteen, and my father fell into a decline after that. He slowly withered away. When he could be stirred to do anything, it was thoughtless and mediocre work. Bad investments and lack of caring to correct our situation led to depleted finances. My father was merely a country squire, but we had been comfortable, and I had no reason to believe that I would have to someday earn my own keep.

"At a time when I should have been going to assemblies and meeting eligible gentlemen appropriate to my station, I was caring for my ailing father and trying to manage the household finances—and failing miserably. When he finally died, the first thing I felt was relief. Relief that it was over. The second thing I felt was guilt. What sort of daughter feels relief that a parent died?"

"He had been sucking away your life, leeching away your youth. It is understandable to feel relief."

"A month after he died, the collectors came. They took everything. I was allowed one bag to carry my clothes, but I was to leave Ridgestone and everything I had known. I sat on the cart, watching my home disappear, and I made two promises. One was to never be in debt to anyone, and the other was to one day return to Ridgestone as its mistress and owner."

"And so when you met Thomas . . ."

"He made me laugh. After so long, it felt so good to just laugh. He reminded me of the joy to be found in life. Our dreams were different, but we worked on a way to accommodate both of us. He said being a gentleman farmer was better than being a butler anyways, and there would be no one to stop him from answering his own door. I felt safe and happy around him, so when he asked for my hand, I said yes."

"But?"

"Two weeks later he died of a fever."

"Oh, my darling." A kiss was pressed to her temple. Fingers brushed away tears she hadn't even realized were falling.

"Lady Allen died a month later herself. The new owners had no need of a companion or a governess, so I made my way to London. I was very fortunate to find a reputable agency willing to take me on and then to have Lady Aldgate offer me this position. And that is how I found myself a governess."

Several minutes passed. Claire continued to stare into the dying fire, the crackling and popping the only sound. She was reluctant to do anything to break the mood but knew that they could not remain as they were forever.

She broke the silence again. "But I won't be a governess forever. I still have the dream of returning to Ridgestone, but it has changed somewhat."

"How so?" He seemed genuinely curious.

"You may find this ridiculous," she warned.

Jacob raised his hand. "I promise to not laugh, on pain of death. Or at least child duty for a whole day."

She smiled at his comment. "There are some other governesses in the area, and we have befriended each other. Once a month we manage to arrange our half days in order to have tea, and try to arrange visits so our children can practice socializing with others. We call ourselves the Governess Club and have made a pact."

Jacob's eyebrows went up. "Indeed?"

"Yes," Claire nodded. "We are saving our money to eventually pool together to buy our own residence and once again become women of means. No more having our lives dictated by others, but to be independent. The initial plan is to regain Ridgestone, but should that fail, we will find another suitable location for all of us."

"That is quite ambitious," Jacob said.

"Well, yes, but we have given ourselves a good time frame. We made this pact six months ago and have given ourselves at least three years to come up with the money."

"It does appear that you are well on your way to organizing this," Jacob agreed and shifted away from her. "On that note, I do believe it is getting late and we should retire. The demons are notorious for rising early and having all of their energy before luncheon."

Claire gave a weak laugh to cover the sudden loss of heat and connection she felt. She, too, moved to her feet. "Yes, they do tend to be energetic in the mornings."

"Very inconsiderate of them. Oh, leave that," Jacob instructed as Claire moved to take the tray down. "This was your special treat, so I will take care of it."

Claire raised her eyebrows at him. "Ten days, and you go from arrogance to cleaning up so the maids won't have to. I must be a better instructor than I thought."

"You, my dear, are magic." The words were softly spoken, and the air crackled between them. Jacob picked up one of the sweetmeats they had neglected and held it to her mouth. "Never forget that."

Without taking her eyes off of his, Claire opened her mouth, and he pushed the sugared treat into it. Having tasted Mrs. Potter's sweetmeats before, Claire was sure it was delicious, but at that moment, all she was aware of was Jacob Knightly.

He lifted his fingers to his mouth and licked off the remaining sugar, never breaking their connected gaze. God in heaven, heat emanated from within her, flushing her skin. Unable to stop herself, she took a shuddering breath.

In response, he winged an arm at her. "Shall I escort you to your door, my lady?"

It was effective enough to break the spell over her, and a

short laugh escaped her. "Thank you, my lord." Slipping her hand into his elbow, they walked the short distance to her room. Once there, she turned to face him. "Thank you for your kind escort, my lord. You are truly a gentleman."

He sketched her an elaborate bow. "The pleasure was all mine, my lady." But when Claire turned to open her door, he caught her elbow. "Thank you, Claire Bannister, for sharing your story. It is an honor to have your trust."

Claire had the same thought as earlier: this man was dangerous, especially when he was sincere. But at that moment, Claire didn't care. Before she could think about stopping herself, she stood on her tiptoes and pressed her lips to his, lingering for a divine moment.

"Good night, Mr. Knightly," she whispered, and disappeared into her room.

CHAPTER FIVE

"Goodness, it's huge!"

Peering through the window, Claire smiled at Michael's exclamation. Light spilled out from the candles in the room, barely illuminating the tutor and his two young charges gathered around his telescope on the small section of roof outside the tutor and governess rooms. Michael was gazing through the device, his hands waving excitedly.

"How does it work?" Michael asked, alternating between peering through the telescope and up at the sky with his naked eye.

"My turn again," Peter demanded, pushing Michael away.

"Not yet!" the other twin yelled, regaining his balance and pushing Peter away from the telescope.

Jacob grabbed each boy by the collar and held them apart. "Neither of you will have another turn if you do not behave appropriately." His voice remained calm and reasonable, matter of fact. "This is an expensive, hard-to-come-by piece of equipment. I would not appreciate it if it was to be broken and that would curtail our astronomical studies."

"My father would buy me a new one," Peter said sullenly.

"Yeah, he can buy the whole world if he wanted to," Michael joined in.

"That is not the point," Jacob said. "Regardless of how much money one has, one must always treat the property of others with care and respect. It is courteous and one of the hallmarks of a gentleman. And Master Peter, Michael had yet to finish his turn; you must learn patience."

"But—"

"No buts. You must learn to be patient. Using force to get what you want is selfish and bullying, a certain way to lose the respect of your peers and colleagues."

"What's a colleague?"

"The people you work with, or choose to spend time with. Peers are something similar, but are made up of your social equals; colleagues can be from all walks of life."

"So Miss Bannister is my colleague?" Michael asked

Jacob chuckled. "No, she is your governess. She is my colleague, because I work with her. Now, back to astronomy. What are star formations called?"

"Constellations." The boys' voices rang together in the darkness.

"Correct. The two constellations I pointed out to you are . . ."

"Ursa Major," said Michael while Peter shouted out, "Ursa Minor."

"And their common names are?"

"The Big Bear and the Little Bear."

"What are the easily recognizable parts?"

"The Big Dipper and the Little Dipper."

"They are not constellations, but . . ."

"Ast—ask—asptker—" It was clearly a new word the boys had difficulty with.

"Asterisms. Shape formations in a constellation are called asterisms," Jacob explained slowly. "Now, look up to the sky and find the Big Dipper."

"Found it!" Michael called out.

"I found it first," Peter cried.

"Did not!"

"It does not matter who found it first, just that both of you found it." Once again, Jacob's voice remained matter of fact. Claire wondered how he managed to maintain his calm. "You both have it in sight?"

"Yes, it's there." Both boys pointed to it.

"Good. Now squeeze your eyes shut and start spinning around. Don't stop spinning until I say."

Whatever is he doing? Claire thought. But the boys obediently started spinning around, giggling as they did so.

"Stop!" Jacob called out. The boys stopped and righted themselves. "Open your eyes and find the Big Dipper." It took them a few moments, but soon both boys were pointing at it. "Again," Jacob commanded. "Close your eyes and spin until I say stop."

Claire watched as he put the boys through the same process three more times. Each time, the boys were successful in pointing out the Big Dipper, although it was clear that by the last time their small bodies were reeling from the activity. Knocking on the glass, she caught Jacob's attention and indicated her timepiece. It would be a good time for the boys to be put to bed; the twins had already been up much later than usual to accommodate the astronomy lesson.

Some time later, Claire entered her private room, having put all the children in their beds and closed up the nursery for the night. She was looking forward to pressing a cool cloth to her neck; the humidity of the season was getting to her, and the cool cloth would help her relax enough to sleep. Safely in the privacy of her room, she made no attempt to stifle her yawn, instead glorying in it as she stood on her tiptoes and stretched her arms out. Lord, what a wonderful feeling.

A grinning face at the window strangled a shriek from her throat. In the odd combination of dark and light, Jacob's head seemed disembodied, floating with no body, adding to the eeriness of the sight.

When she heard his laughter through the window, Claire's fright turned to pique. She marched to the window and pushed it open. "It is just like you to spy through a lady's window."

Unrepentant, Jacob leaned folded arms across the windowsill. "You're the one who left her curtains open. A man can only be so good."

Claire leaned down and mimicked his stance at the windowsill, her arms running the length of his. "Is that the best you can do, blame your inherently sinful masculine nature?" She saw his eyes lower to her mouth, perilously close to his, and knew he was remembering her all-too-brief kiss two nights prior. Every time she had a moment to herself she found that evening by the fire replaying over and over through her mind, each sensation dancing over her skin again. A few times she had even lost track of the lesson she had been teaching, which spoke to the level of her distraction.

And she was distracted now. By his nearness, by his focus

on her mouth, by the scent of him. Would he kiss her again? Did she want him to? Her blood pounded out a resounding yes.

But he disappointed her. He straightened from the window and held out his hand to her. "Join me for some stargazing."

The prospect was so appealing she didn't even mind his imperious phrasing. Sitting on the windowsill, she allowed him to help her down on to the roof. It wasn't that high of a jump, but Jacob held her hips firmly as he helped her down. When her feet touched the graveled surface, his hands remained on her hips and she swayed toward him.

This time he took advantage of her willingness and pressed his lips to hers.

The feel of his strong lips moving against hers was too much to resist. Perhaps females had inherently sinful natures too, for all Claire wanted to do was press herself against his strong body, preferably naked. She contented herself with sliding her arms around his neck and moving close enough to feel the texture of his coat press against her dress. It had been four years since she had truly kissed a man, but the knowledge flooded back, and she moved her lips in time with his.

Their breathing quickened and their tongues began to flick and trace and explore each other's mouths. Jacob's tongue ran underneath her lower lip, dragging it into his mouth and gently sucking. A small whimper of delight rose in her and her fingers slid into his hair, relishing the silky feeling of it between her fingers. Claire rose on her tiptoes to gain better access to his mouth.

Heat fused through her body as whorls of sensation emanated from her mouth, traveling down her body. Jacob finally moved his hands, wrapping one arm around her back while the other hand slid down to cup her bottom and tilted her into his pelvis, kneading as he did so.

Claire could not mistake the evidence of his desire. Pressed against her belly, she could feel the bulge continue to swell and grow, and she felt an answering wetness gather between her legs.

As much as her body screamed at her to continue this to completion, the small part of her mind that remained rational became incessantly vocal. With a moan, she broke the kiss. "Stop," she gasped.

"Soon," Jacob muttered, burying his head in her neck. Her eyes closed as he began to nuzzle her neck, little nips teasing her skin.

"But the stars . . ."

"Hang the stars." He took her mouth again, sliding his tongue inside to dance with hers. Little mewls of appreciation vibrated up her throat.

But again, she broke the kiss. "Stop."

"Soon."

"Now." She accompanied that with a small push against his chest.

With a sigh, Jacob loosened his embrace and leaned back slightly. Breathing hard, he pressed his forehead against hers. Sweet Mary, but he wanted her. Wanted her so bad his every pore ached for her. Every nerve in his body was currently thrumming with unfulfilled desire and all from a mere chaste kiss, at least compared to what he wanted to do to her. What was it about this woman?

"Magic," he breathed, his heart resuming its normal pace. Dropping a kiss to her forehead, he stepped away and winged an elbow at her. "My lady, your stars await."

"Miss Bannister!"

The high-pitched annoyance in the child's tone finally broke Claire out of her reverie. Blinking, she saw the angry faces of Miss Sophie and Miss Mary glaring at her. Miss Allison was playing with her dolls in the corner, unaware of her sisters' annoyance.

"My apologies; I was woolgathering," Claire said. "Is something the matter?"

Miss Sophie crossed her arms and made an unladylike sound. "You were staring off into space. You were talking about stargazing and then just stopped."

"We called your name four times," Miss Mary added, holding up her fingers for emphasis.

Claire felt her face burn hot. How could she confess to her charges the nature of her thoughts? She couldn't, of course. She cleared her throat. "Of course. Mr. Knightly has promised to show you how to use his telescope to look at the stars more closely."

"I fail to see what is interesting about stars," Sophie said, her nose tilted at the angle only eleven-year-olds could manage.

How little she knows, Claire thought to herself. Her thoughts went back to that kiss she and Mr. Knightly shared outside her window. Days later, it still made her body tingle. Then later, standing beside him in the darkness, his coat keeping her warm and his arm a comforting weight across her shoulders as he pointed out the names of different stars. If he asked her now, she wouldn't be able to recall any of those names, but describing the sensation of being held by him? She could write a whole book on that. His arm had been draped lazily, but possessively, warming her . . .

"MISS BANNISTER!"

Good heavens, she must get hold of herself. "My apologies again, ladies." Taking a deep breath, she thought of how to distract them. "It appears that this is meant to be a leisure day. Shall we spend the afternoon at the lake?"

Squeals followed her suggestion, and skirts flurried around small legs. With a smile, Claire rose to her feet and addressed the maid waiting in the corner. "Lucy, could you fetch towels please?"

"Of course, Miss Bannister."

"Would you like to join us?" Claire asked as Lucy made her way to the door.

"Thanks fer the offer, Miss, but if ye don't mind, I'd be takin' this time ta tidy up in a ways I can't when the children are underfoot."

"I understand. Could you bring a picnic basket out in a couple of hours? I am sure the girls would enjoy a cold luncheon this afternoon. It is so gorgeous out today." Claire moved to her room to change into her swimming dress.

"Of course, Miss," Lucy replied. "And fer the young masters?"

"I don't know where Mr. Knightly has taken them," Claire said. "We will simply have to wait for their return." She was unsure of how to interpret what his absence made her feel.

An hour later, Claire sat on the grass, sunning herself as she watched the girls play in the water. Her hair was beginning to dry and frizzle around her head, but she didn't care; being out of doors on such a day was a treat. She could always wash and brush her hair later. She tilted her head back to catch more of the sun's rays, smiling at the playful shrieks coming from the water.

A call from the direction of the house captured her attention. Shielding her eyes from the sun, Claire saw Jacob walking toward the lake with the two boys, swinging a picnic basket at his side. Peter and Michael were already pulling off their coats and shoes, their eyes eagerly on the play in the lake. With barely a greeting to her, they discarded their shirts and pants, rushing to the shore in only their smalls, their shrieks as high-pitched as their sisters'.

Jacob grinned at her as he stopped close to her side. Gazing down at her tilted face and outstretched legs, a bolt of lust rushed through his body. Since that night on the roof, his dreams had been haunted by the memory of her lips and body against his, causing him to wake in uncomfortable states. One night he even embarrassed himself when he saw the stain on the sheets. "We intercepted Lucy on her way from the nursery," he said, indicating the basket. "A leisure day seems well in order." He dropped the basket on the ground and knelt down, his head cocked to the side. "To think, I have never actually seen a bird with its feathers ruffled; now I have no need to."

Claire frowned at him. "What do you mean?"

He reached out and tugged her frizzy hair. "Just that, birdie." He grinned as she swatted his hand away. "Coming for a swim?" He straightened and started pulling off his clothing.

The ability to think deserted her. Claire stared as his physique was revealed, one piece of clothing at a time. When he began to pull his shirt out of his pantaloons, breathing was forgotten. Good heavens, had she actually pressed herself against that? Did all men's chests look like that? Claire could not stop herself from staring at the muscles dancing across his torso and abdomen as he finished stripping off his shirt. Light curly hair carpeted his chest, tapering down until it disappeared beneath his . . .

Heavens, was he going to remove his pantaloons as well? Claire felt faint but could not move, could not swallow, could not breathe. All she could do was stare and silently beg him to not stop at his pantaloons.

"Are you going to swim?" His repeated question jerked her out of her trance. Claire felt her face burn with embarrassment at her thoughts.

"Miss Bannister." Claire was grateful for young Allison's interruption. Not only did it keep her from having to speak to Jacob before she had composed herself, it gave her something to look at other than his magnificent chest. A chest that would put Michelangelo's *David* to shame, a chest that all the gods on Olympus would envy, a chest that . . .

Dear heavens, there she went again, writing a book about the man.

"Yes, Miss Allison?" she asked.

"I don't want to swim no more."

"I suppose that answers my question," Jacob said. He gave her a half-smile and let his gaze linger appreciatively on her legs before heading to the water to join the other children.

Claire watched as he walked away, knowing she should feel ashamed for taking such pleasure in the sight, but she felt no such thing. Heavens, but his backside was glorious.

Lucy had a secretive smile on her face as she slid into her seat for tea. Claire looked at her with a raised brow as she handed Jacob his cup. "Don't you look like a cat that has been in the cream," she teased. "What is it?" She poured the maid a tea, adding the extras she liked.

Lucy just grinned some more. "Somethin' I know yer gonna like," she said in a singsong voice.

Claire smiled back, the maid's excitement infectious. "What is it?" she asked again.

Lucy took a generous sip of her tea. "What is something' ye enjoy mightily but canna do very often?"

Claire let out a laugh. "There are many things that fall into that category, Lucy." She stole a look at Jacob sitting back in his chair, watching the two friends. *And many new things that fall into that category as well.* Jacob glanced her way, and the look he gave her made Claire think he could read her very thoughts. A flush of heat stole across her face, and she turned her attention back to Lucy.

"But this is somethin' that none of us gets to do lots, not if yer not part of the toffs. You've told me lots of stories about these."

Suspicious comprehension blossomed in her mind. Claire studied her friend's excitement, difficult to suppress. "You mean . . ."

"Yes," Lucy burst out, unable to contain herself anymore. She slipped a parchment from her bosom where it had been folded up and handed it to Claire. She unfolded it and read it. "A servant's assembly, in just three days' time," the maid practically sang. "It took some sweet talkin', but Mr. Fosters and Mrs. Morrison finally said the younger staff can go. That includes you two," she finished, with a smiling nod toward Jacob.

Jacob straightened in his chair, interest plain on his face. "An assembly? With dancing and such?"

Claire smiled at him. "Yes, we do know how to dance here in the country," she teased.

He smiled back, leaning toward her. "I never assumed otherwise, my lady. I am merely overcome with the thought of seeing you traipse across the floor."

Claire couldn't stop the flush from covering her face. She watched as Jacob followed the flush as it disappeared below her neckline, causing the blush to deepen even more. He chuckled deeply.

Claire looked back at Lucy, noticing the maid watching them with barely concealed interest. She cleared her throat and sat up straighter. "Have you heard of any other households attending, Lucy?"

With a knowing smile, Lucy replied, "Not yet, Miss, but I'm sure there's lots of excitement. I'm to the market tomorrow, and I'll see what I can pick up."

"And I'll be sure to have my dancing shoes polished," Jacob said. "It's been quite some time since I've had the pleasure of a country assembly."

Claire looked at him. "Are there none in Oxford or Cambridge?"

Jacob shrugged. "How would I know? I'm from London. Haven't spent much time outside of the city for years."

Claire was confused. "Then where did you study?"

Jacob stared at her. How could he have let such a simple mistake slip? Of course a tutor would have some university training in him. And he did attend Oxford, on paper at least.

He cleared his throat. "Oxford, briefly, but most of my education was from my uncle. He is a rector and took a sabbatical for several years from his parish at my father's behest. It was cheaper than university." That, and he had been sent down so many times they refused to let him return. It was his father's youngest brother who had taken him on and engendered a decent respect for certain studies. "And while I was there, country assemblies weren't an activity that garnered my interest."

"And now they are?" Claire asked with a raised brow.

"It's been an age since we've danced at an assembly," Lucy said. With a giggle, she grabbed Claire's hands and pulled her up. Without hesitating, Claire bowed to Lucy's curtsey and they began to dance a Scottish reel. Unable to resist their excitement, Jacob began to whistle a tune and slap his knees, providing music and a rhythm.

The women laughed their way around the room, their skirts whirling with their movements. Jacob was mesmerized by the sight of Claire's face, giddy and flushed, her eyes sparkling with delight. It was not as though she was? an unhappy person, but Jacob had yet to see her experience this kind of pleasure. It radiated off her, the waves nearly visible as they filled the room. He could feel them move around him; the hairs on his arms tingled.

Good Lord, but he needed her. Needed to bed her. It had become more than just a spot of fun; it had grown into an obsession. He wanted her . . . presence, for lack of a better word. He was honest with himself to recognize his selfishness. He wanted it in his life to bring him happiness, to possibly bring him the fulfillment he knew was lacking in his life. If he could somehow . . . learn it from her . . . perhaps he would finally be able to begin being his own man.

If he could somehow tie her to him, somehow guarantee that she would remain in his life, then even if he couldn't learn it her presence would continue to enrich his life. It would mean more than just bedding her, of course. It meant marriage. Surprisingly, the thought of such a thing didn't send chills down his spine as it had in the past. Rather, the primitive male side of him rejoiced at that thought, for it meant multiple and repeated beddings with such an amazing woman.

And given how much she enjoyed dancing, the servants' assembly was the time to make his move.

CHAPTER SIX

"**O**oee, miss, ye've done gone and made me look lovely." Lucy turned her head and lightly fingered the upswept arrangement Claire had set her hair in. Dressed in a simple green dress, Lucy did indeed look lovely.

Claire smiled at Lucy in the mirror. "Lovely enough to perhaps catch Alfred's eye even." She laughed as a light blush stole over Lucy's cheeks.

"Do ye really think so?" Lucy looked hopeful.

"If he doesn't," Claire said, "then he doesn't deserve you, dear."

"Oh, but miss, he's so handsome," Lucy protested, turning around and looking at Claire. "And he's been lookin' and talkin' so sweet to me these past weeks. He even tol' me that he'd not like seeing me dance wit' other blokes tonight."

Claire sat on Lucy's bed and looked at her friend. She knew that servants were held to a different code than the nobility; the strictures between men and women were more lax. Claire thought of Jacob and felt a stab of envy hit her stomach. "Lucy, if you aren't sure about his intentions, do not let him talk you into anything you feel uncomfortable with."

Lucy smiled at her. "This ain't my first time with a gent, miss. If we does it right, I'll be getting' jes' as much out of it as Alfie. I don't have ideas for anythin' more."

Claire had difficulty fathoming such an attitude. "But do you not want more?"

"Maybe." Lucy shrugged. She looked back in the mirror and tucked a stray tendril behind her ear. "I don't say I'd not like a man and wee ones of me own. But I've got time yet, so I figger I can have me some fun while waitin'." She gave Claire a cheeky smile before sobering again. "And I don't see nothin' wrong with a gent and a girl doin' somethin' if they both want it. We ain't special, miss; we ain't like the toffs. I see the way you and Mr. Knightly be lookin' at each other. I say that if ye be feelin' anything for Mr. Knightly like what I feels for Alfie, then I says ye need to stop thinkin' like the squire's daughter ye was raised as."

Claire stared down at her hands. Here she thought to give Lucy advice regarding Alfred, but instead her friend imparted some wisdom to her. It was true; she was no longer a squire's daughter, no longer special. Perhaps it was time she stopped to holding to such illusions. Not give up everything completely, but merely alter her viewpoint slightly.

All her life she had been raised to believe that purity was the highest commodity a woman could have. Yet as Lucy just pointed out, she was no longer in the class of people who held firmly to that value. Was this possible? Could she actually do this? What would she be risking?

Her job. Her reputation. Even if she acknowledged that it was not as precious as it used to be, risking her reputation could have detrimental effects on the Governess Club's future. She wasn't naïve; she knew the risks. Becoming with child would seriously jeopardize the Club's plans. She would not be able to remain with her friends, not if they were to have any chance of success. Could she risk the hopes, the ambitions, the future of her friends?

"Miss," Lucy caught her attention. "Yer thinkin' too much about it."

Claire raised her eyes to Lucy's. "There is so much at risk."

Lucy smiled sympathetically and shrugged. "Only in yer head, Miss. And if somethin' does happen, well, ye figger it out then."

Claire bit her lips, still uncertain.

Lucy patted her hands. "I knows some ways to help his seed from catchin' ye, if ye'd like me ta tell ye. They may not be perfect, but they help."

After only a brief hesitation, Claire nodded and silently said goodbye to her former self.

Entering the assembly room, the servants from Aldgate Hall were greeted with stuffy air and the scent of sweat. Dancing had already started; flushed faces were testament to the heat, exertion and excitement. The sight and noise was unlike anything one would see in a London ballroom; there, ennui and detachment reigned, not this enthusiastic participation.

Jacob turned to ask Claire to dance, only to find her being whisked away from the group by a fresh-faced fellow. He watched in disbelief as Claire laughed and smiled at the young man. An uncomfortable annoyance began to build in his stomach as Jacob continued to watch the man with his—*his*—Claire. He didn't even look like a fully grown man, more of a boy trying to look like a man, with slicked-back hair and tight cravat. He doubted the boy was even old enough to shave; there were still spots on his face, for Christ's sake. Why would Claire consent to dance with him, let alone smile at him in such a way?

A tug on his sleeve managed to pull his attention away from the dance floor. Lucy raised her eyebrows at the ferocity of his glare when it was turned on her. She gave him a lopsided smile. "C'mon Mr. Knightly. Dance wit' me instead of glarin' at Thomas."

Jacob scowled even more. "His name is Thomas?" Claire's dead betrothed's name was Thomas. Perhaps she had a penchant for men with that name.

"Come on," Lucy insisted. This time Jacob allowed himself to be dragged onto the dance floor. They joined the dancers mid-set. Jacob tried to keep his eyes on Claire and Baby Thomas, but it was difficult with all the whirling bodies crammed into such a small space.

"Mr. Knightly," Lucy said, "see tha' man over there?" She indicated a tall, strapping man with curly blond hair that resembled a mop standing on the edge of the dance floor, arms crossed, feet set apart in a fighter's stance and glaring at him so fiercely that Jacob wouldn't be surprised if the air between them burst into flame.

"Who's he?" Jacob asked, turning his back on the potent glare. "And why is he trying to kill me with his eyes?"

Lucy grinned and looked at the man. "Alfie. He's a stable boy at the Beecham estate. He's sweet on me."

"Why are you telling me this?"

"Cos' he's lookin' at ye the way ye be lookin' at Thomas. He don't like me dancin' wit' other blokes neither."

Jacob looked at Lucy and raised a brow. "I do not look like that." He looked over the dancers, trying to spot Claire again.

"Yes, ye do. Yer the one who didn't ask her to dance fast enough. Jes' like Alfie."

"That is a mistake I will never repeat," Jacob said, still scanning the crowd. The music had ended, and the dancers were beginning to dissipate. Jacob caught a glimpse of Claire's pink dress making its way to the refreshment table on the arm of Baby Thomas. "Come," he said, taking Lucy's arm and tugging her in the same direction.

Lucy resisted. "Mr. Knightly, I think I'll be goin' over to Alfie now."

Jacob stopped and glanced between the maid and the scowling stable boy. The man hadn't moved with the ending of the music. Knowing he was taking a risk, he leaned over and whispered in Lucy's ear. "Never go to him; make him come to you. Now smile like I said something sweet and flirtatious."

Lucy smiled at him like she was born to the stage. She slipped her arm through Jacob's and said, "Yes, lemonade would be lovely."

Right. Enough was enough. The first dance, he had been too slow to ask her. He understood that. The second dance—he could allow even that. It was crowded, after all. But the fourth dance? Unacceptable. For four dances, Jacob had to watch Claire spin and sashay and smile at her dance partners.

All at her dance partners, not at him. At the rate this was going, his scowl was going to freeze onto his face.

Even Alfie hadn't made Lucy wait long into the second dance. And here he still was, cooling his heels on the edge of the dance floor, watching Claire spend her time with other men. If he didn't know better, he would think she was deliberately taunting him.

He didn't like it. Not one iota. Even now, halfway through the fourth set, his teeth were aching from the grinding. And he still had at least ten more minutes until the set ended. He was considering forgetting his gentleman training and striding onto the floor to claim what was his.

"She has always been popular at assemblies and other gatherings."

Jacob turned to the soft, cultured voice at his elbow. A woman who could not be much more than twenty stood beside him, gazing out onto the dance floor. Her blond hair was swept up into a simple yet elegant coif that accentuated her slender neck. Glancing at him with intelligent brown eyes, Jacob was given a clear view of her gently rounded face and classic nose. His gaze involuntarily swept downwards, taking in the quality of her dress, despite its age. Returning his gaze to hers, Jacob was sure of one thing: she was out of place here.

"I beg your pardon?" he asked.

She smiled. "Miss Bannister. She has an innate kindness and vivaciousness that draws people to her, both men and women. She never lacks for partners in whatever she does."

"You know her well?"

"I have known Claire for over two years. We see each other regularly for tea, so yes, I would say I know her well."

Jacob looked back at Claire on the dance floor. Good, she was still there. "You must be a member of the Governess Club."

"And you must be the new tutor," the young lady rejoined.

Jacob bowed to her. "Mr. Jacob Knightly, at your service."

"Do you not approve of our endeavor, Mr. Knightly? Your tone indicated you do not."

"Does my opinion matter to you?"

"Men seem to be threatened by things they cannot control. Soon there will be four women beyond the control of men as much as they can be. Does that not threaten you?"

Jacob turned to face the young lady fully. "Who are you?"

She gave him a half-smile. "A friend of Miss Bannister's. I will not stand in the way of her happiness, but neither will I countenance her being hurt."

"What makes you think I am going to hurt Cla—Miss Bannister?"

Her smile turned sad. "It is difficult to act contrary to our natures, Mr. Knightly. I pray that you prove to be different, but only time will tell." She glanced out at the dancers. "The music is ending. You will not want to move too slowly this time."

Jacob turned to look for Claire as well; sure enough, the set was finishing. He looked back to impart one final comment to the young lady, but all he saw was her moving away and disappearing into the crowd.

Without another thought, Jacob plowed onto the dance floor, to where Claire was curtseying to her partner. He grabbed her wrist. "You must be hot from your dancing. Come outside and cool down."

"Mr. Knightly," Claire began.

"Claire." Both his tone and the look in his eyes held a warning. Claire quickly thanked her partner and succumbed to Jacob's tugging.

"What has gotten into you?" she asked as they left the assembly room. Their footsteps echoed on the wooden steps leading down to the public room. Jacob didn't say anything as he led her outside.

"Is there a garden nearby?" he asked, his tone brusque.

"Yes, just behind the church." Claire pointed the way. She gave a little squeak as he tugged on her wrist again and strode in the direction she indicated. She scrambled to keep up. "Could you please shorten your strides?" He did so infinitesimally.

Jacob didn't seem able to draw an easy breath until he had led Claire into the small garden. It was difficult to see everything in the moonlight, but a small circular pathway around the flowers was visible, including a pair of benches. When he finally stopped, Claire pulled her wrist out of his hand.

"What has gotten into you?" she asked again.

Jacob turned toward her. "I don't like being ignored," he growled.

"I wasn't ignoring you."

"No? Then how many dances have you shared with me? None. And how many with that groom of yours? Two, Claire. There's only been four dances so far, and half have gone to the upstart who can't grow a beard."

"Thomas? I suppose you may be right. I've never seen him with any facial hair, but that is no cause to disparage him."

"I will disparage whomever I please."

"And if you had asked me to dance, I would have said yes," Claire pointed out.

"I tried to." Jacob was still growling at her. "But I can't seem to get close enough, thanks to your male harem."

"My what?" Claire gasped.

"Every boy in the country who is old enough to know what's what is slavering after you. And you encourage it, with your smiles and your laughter and your dancing."

"How dare you?" she breathed.

Jacob began to advance on her. "Even your blond friend deemed fit to comment on your popularity and how you never seem to lack for partners, whatever the activity."

"Louisa?" Claire asked confused, instinctively moving away from his approach. "She would never insinuate—"

"She didn't have to." Jacob continued to advance on her. "I saw it with my own two eyes. The way they look at you. The way they want to touch you. And it's all because of what you do."

Claire felt the back of her legs hit one of the stone benches. "What do I do?"

Jacob threaded his hand into her hair, grasping her head firmly. "You smile at them. You talk with them. You laugh with them. You dance with them. You make them feel like they are the most important man in the room. All this you have been doing tonight. But not to me."

Claire stared at him, dumbfounded. "Are you jealous?" she asked in a whisper.

His eyes narrowed. "I dislike you dancing with other men," he muttered before crushing his lips to hers.

This was not like the other kisses they had shared. There

was no teasing, no gentleness, no seduction. This kiss was pure domination. His lips pried hers open and his tongue invaded her mouth. Claire couldn't catch her breath from the force of his attentions. She tried to twist her head to rectify her lack of oxygen, but it only resulted in his tightening the arm around her waist and the hand in her hair.

Claire did the only thing she could think of, the thing her body began to urge her to do. This was Jacob after all, the man she had come to respect and care about. She knew him, knew that this behavior was out of character for him. She had no qualms doing what needed to be done.

Claire began to kiss him back, moving his lips against his, trying to match his movements. Despite his grip, Claire managed to press her hands against his chest. She could feel his heart beating hard through the layers of his clothing. Was it from anger or passion?

A small moan escaped him, and Claire slid her arms up to his shoulders and around his neck, pressing her body against his. Jacob's kiss began to gentle, reducing the painful pressure on her mouth and eliciting small tendrils of pleasure in her lips that swirled down her throat.

"Claire," he murmured.

"Jacob," she sighed as he moved away from her lips and began to trail kisses along her cheek and down her throat. She tilted her head to give him more access. His hands trailed along her back before settling on the cheeks of her bottom, cupping them and pulling her hips into his pelvis. There was no mistaking his reaction to her.

Claire's throat went dry. Thomas, her former betrothed, had taken some liberties, but nothing like this. Her body was discovering sensations it had never known existed before this moment.

And then his hand moved upward to cup her breast. Her eyes flew open and slid half shut again. "Jacob," she croaked.

"Claire." She felt his voice against her skin.

With a final nibble where her neck met her collarbone, Jacob captured her mouth again, inhaling her gasps. Lord, but he was quickly becoming addicted to her.

He guided her down to sit on the stone bench, following her down to kneel on the ground in front of her. He nudged her legs opened with his hips and moved in closer. With a growl, he tugged her skirt up enough to settle in completely in the cradle of her thighs. Even this close felt like heaven.

But a dark church garden was not the place. With strength of will he hadn't known he possessed, he broke the kiss and pressed his forehead against hers.

"Don't do that again."

"What?" He could see the glaze lingering in her eyes.

"Not dance with me."

Claire cupped his cheeks, running her thumbs over his cheekbones. She could feel the small hairs of a new beard tickle her palms. It was a new experience she wouldn't mind having again and again. Just like his kisses. Just like being with him.

Oh heavens, she had done gone and fallen in love with him, to borrow Lucy's phrase.

She smiled at him. "Was that your way of asking me to dance, Mr. Knightly?"

"Just don't do it again. You are mine."

Claire leaned into him and kissed him again. This time it was her tongue that pushed into his mouth. This time it was she who drank in his deep moans, she who pushed her pelvis into his. Heavens, what pleasure.

One hand caressed a breast, kneading and shaping it, his thumb teasing her nipple. His other hand went to the hem of her skirt and disappeared underneath it. He didn't stop to stroke her thigh, he didn't stop to play with the undoubtedly sensible drawers and chemise. No, he unerringly found the juncture at her thighs and cupped it, pressing his palm in hard.

Sweet Jesus, but she was responsive. He had expected her to panic and close up. Instead, the pressure from his palm tore a little squeak from her and her legs opened wider. He slid a finger inside of her, feeling her wetness coat his hand.

Claire jerked against him and moaned.

"You are mine, Claire. Say it."

"Jacob."

"Say it."

"I am yours." Her head fell back and her body arched into his hand. Jacob put his free arm around her back to support her. Jacob increased his pressure and motions. Her body began to convulse, her inner muscles tightening around his fingers. A few moments later, small cries came from her in tandem with the pulsing of her release. He captured her cries with his mouth, swallowing each sweet taste.

Claire came back to earth, and Jacob pulled his hand away from her. Her body spent, she leaned her forehead against his shoulder, trying to regain her senses.

"You are mine, Claire." Jacob's voice was hoarse.

"Yes."

"We will return to the assembly," he said, kissing her hair. "You will dance with me. And when we return to Aldgate Hall, I will come to your room tonight."

Claire did not hesitate. "Yes."

CHAPTER SEVEN

Jacob pressed his ear to the wall separating his room from Claire's. He couldn't hear a thing. Upon returning to Aldgate Hall, they had each retired to their respective chambers to prepare themselves. Hell, he hadn't needed preparation at all, but felt she may need a few more moments to settle what was going to happen in her mind.

And it made up for his earlier lack of finesse. *I will come to your room tonight?* He couldn't remember ever being so awkward. Ladies—women—enjoyed sweet words and being wooed. But seeing Claire share even one dance with another man had Jacob losing his senses and control. *I will come to your room tonight* indeed.

With a sigh, Jacob pushed himself away from the wall. He didn't know how long she would need to prepare herself, but he couldn't wait any longer. And if she wasn't ready, didn't want to go through with this tonight, then he would play the gentleman and acquiesce to her wishes.

Wearing only his shirt and trousers, he moved to her door and knocked. She didn't leave him waiting even a moment, but opened the door. Her hair was tied back in a braid that Jacob's fingered itched to release; his hands tingled with the memory of its softness from earlier in the evening. She was dressed in her night rail, a long cotton garment that covered her from her neck to the top of her feet, material so thick and practical that the glow of the candles behind her did not penetrate it. She was beautiful.

As he promised himself, he played the gentleman. "You don't—that is, we don't have to—if you don't want to or have doubts—"

She interrupted him. "Jacob. Come in." She reached out and took his hand, welcoming him into her room.

The door closed behind him with a small squeak. He made sure to twist the lock in place; he hadn't forgotten that much at least. Coherent thought fled as he looked at her, standing so demure, so willing, so glorious. His blood thudded heavily through his veins; he had trouble deciding what to do first.

"I have done this before," he blurted out.

A shy, awkward half smile appeared on her face. "I have not."

Dammit, what was wrong with him? "I meant to say that I usually have more finesse. But you—I can't seem to think around you."

"Oh." She contemplated his statement before continuing. "Lucy said that some people leave their garments on while others do not. Which one do you prefer?"

Was she serious? If he wasn't so far gone with arousal, he would find the situation humorous. Him, being helped by a virgin. Perhaps later he would chuckle about it.

"I want you to know that my intentions are honorable, Claire. You are not a dalliance to me."

Her eyes softened. "Thank you."

Sweet Jesus, he could get used to that look in her eyes. Full of trust and openness and affection, all directed at him. He could not recall a time that anyone had looked at him in such a manner. It was humbling and arousing. Frightening even, to be the recipient of such faith.

"Claire." He moved toward her and cupped her cheeks.

She smiled tremulously, her nerves showing. A shaky giggle escaped her. "Our conversation in these situations leaves much to be desired."

"It is not your conversation I desire at this moment," he replied. He lowered his head and kissed her.

She didn't know where all her hesitation had gone, but since her conversation with Lucy earlier, she felt like a different woman. Her decision to leave her past behind had lifted something from her, a heavy cloak or a chain; she felt free, especially with Jacob.

She welcomed his kiss. She opened her mouth eagerly to his seeking tongue and wrapped her arms around his neck, pressing her body against his. She reveled in the feeling of her breasts brushing against his hard chest. She felt the same bulge that had been present in the church garden pushing into her stomach.

He tugged at the ties holding her night rail closed at her neck. "Off," he said against her mouth.

"What?" Her senses had quickly scattered.

"I prefer your garments off."

"Oh." Claire stepped back.

He had never actually seen a woman transform into a seductress before. Where had his proper Claire gone? In her stead was a woman who looked at him from beneath her lashes with knowing eyes while slowly undoing the ribbon at her neck. When it was undone, her night rail gapped so broadly that all it took was a shrug and roll of her shoulders to have it whisper to the floor, slithering down her body.

His mouth went dry at the sight of a nude Claire standing before him. His eyes instinctively settled on the light curls covering her mound; he licked his lips in anticipation.

"Jacob?" Her voice betrayed some of her trepidation.

Raising his eyes back to hers, he quickly shucked his own clothing, feeling the eagerness of an adolescent.

Her eyes widened. A naked Jacob overwhelmed her senses, making him seem too big for the small room. Statues and pictures in forbidden books from her father's collection had not prepared her for such an experience. And he was all hers; no other woman was to see him thus.

She looked into his eyes. "You are mine, Jacob."

"You are mine, Claire," he echoed. He closed the gap between them and lifted her braid off her back. "May I?" he asked. At her nod, he untwisted the tie holding it together and ran his fingers through her hair, loosening the silken strands to spread along her back. "Beautiful," he breathed, the delicate tendrils twining themselves around his fingers.

She slid her arms around his waist and lifted her head to receive his kiss. His hands spread over her back, their weight warm and heavy against her bare skin, sending thrills coursing through her nerves. She felt a reverence in his touch that made her knees weak.

As if sensing her need, he guided her to lie down on her bed, the old frame groaning under their combined weight. It was only meant to hold one person, but neither of them was complaining about the close quarters.

His attentions moved down her body. She arched into his hands, his mouth, her begging silent. He didn't disappoint. His hands worked magic on her skin, her breasts, teasing her senses into pleasurable oblivion.

She could not remain passive. Her fingers itched to know him and caressed his skin in much the same manner. Their moans and gasps created a symphony of pleasure in her tiny room.

When he moved his hand to cup her, he knew he could not last much longer. Her warm wetness beckoned to him and the urge to mount her grew to extreme necessity. He would not be able to do everything to her he desired this time, but there would be ample opportunity in the future. He was sure of it.

Preparing her with his fingers, he moved into the cradle of her thighs and kissed her deeply. "Claire," he groaned.

"Jacob," was her answering gasp as she felt the tip of his hardness at her entrance.

"I'm sorry," he said and pushed deeply into her.

A small cry tore from her throat and he stilled. Her body tensed around his, an instinctive reaction to the pain. He could feel her inner muscles throb and clench around him and he had to grit his teeth against the urge to move. He would wait until she was ready for him, even if it killed him.

"Claire?"

"Jacob." A whimper remained in her voice.

"I am sorry, my lady." He kissed her eyes, tasting the saltiness of unshed tears.

"It is not your doing," she managed. "It happens to every woman."

He chuckled at the revelation he held in his arms. Even at a moment of such personal discomfort, she sought to ease his own suffering. He kissed her deeply, coaxing a response out of her.

When he felt her begin to relax, he yielded a small amount to instinct and rocked against her. Her gasp fluttered over his lips and her body tensed again, but this time he could tell it was not quite from pain. He repeated the movement. This time her hips arched off the bed to meet his, and he knew the moments of discomfort had passed.

He did not surrender himself entirely to his instinct; such selfishness would only cause her more pain, and he refused to make her first experience one she looked back upon with displeasure.

It wasn't long before small squeaks of pleasure bubbled up from her throat; he instinctively recognized them as the hallmark of her impending release. Scant moments later, she arched her body and her head fell back, her mouth open in a silent cry.

Her muscles contracted around his manhood, and he allowed himself to slip into his own release after a few more thrusts. "Claire," he groaned as he spilled into her. He laid his head on her shoulder, inhaling deeply against her neck.

"Jacob," she whispered, hugging him to her.

Silence enveloped them, blanketing the couple with satisfied intimacy. *Life is good*, was his thought as he drifted off to sleep in her embrace.

"**W**hy do you call me 'my lady'?" Thanks to the close quarters of her bed, Jacob was currently spooned behind her. Sometime earlier he had rolled off of her and adjusted himself into the position, pulling her coverlet over them to fend off the crispiness of the night. His solid form behind her both comforted and warmed her, the lazy kisses he was dropping on her shoulder sending quivers along her skin. A lone tallow candle remained flickering on the stand that held her washbasin.

"You have as much grace and poise as any lady I have ever met, so why wouldn't I call you that?" His voice reflected the same satiation as she felt coursing through her veins. "Besides, I like the thought of you being 'my lady'."

Claire smiled at the thought and teased, "You have met so many ladies in your life that you can make an accurate comparison?"

His body tensed behind her. It was infinitesimal, but they were so close she noticed it. "I have met my share," he finally said.

Claire turned to face him, tangling her legs around his and placing a hand on his chest.. Tufts of dark hair spotted Jacob's torso and she ran her fingers through them. She smiled at his inhalation when her fingers brushed over his nipples. "Should I be calling you 'my lord' then?"

Jacob grabbed her hand and raised it to his lips, kissing her palm. "No. To you I am and always will be Jacob. Never 'my lord'."

Her brow furrowed at his fierce and adamant tone. Why wouldn't he let her play the game as well? She brushed off her misgivings for a more serious matter. "But not in public, Jacob. We must be discreet; our positions demand it."

Jacob laid her hand back on his chest. "I said earlier that my intentions were honorable, Claire. This is not a dalliance to me. I wish to marry you." He was surprised at the sincerity that rang in his voice and was struck by the truth of his words. He did want to marry her for pure reasons, not merely manipulate her into it.

He wanted to marry her because he loved her. Never had anything felt so right as the thought of loving her, marrying her. "Will you do me the honor of becoming my wife, Claire Bannister?"

Claire stared at her hand on his chest covered by his hand. Her silence unnerved him. Did she not reciprocate his feelings? Was everything he saw in her eyes and experienced in her bed a lie? At the thought, Jacob felt a gaping hole open where his stomach used to be.

Claire bit her lip and looked to his eyes. "What about the Governess Club? My friends are depending on me."

Jacob forced himself to keep his tone level. "Surely they will not begrudge you your happiness."

"Will I be happy with you?"

"I will do my utmost to ensure you are never unhappy, my lady." He raised her hand to his lips again. "I love you, Claire." The words flowed easily. He had always assumed that if he ever did fall in love, saying the phrase would be awkward and arduous, as in the novels women read. But no, saying them felt right and natural, like pulling on a pair of well-worn, comfortable boots. Loving Claire just . . . fit.

She smiled broadly at him. "I love you as well, Jacob. And yes, I will marry you. I will make you the happiest man alive."

Jacob let out a crow that had Claire quickly covering his

mouth. "Shh," she admonished. "We cannot have the house-hold coming in here."

"But we are betrothed, my lady," he said, unable to stop grinning. "Let them find us. Let the entire country come into this room right now. I don't care."

"Silly man." Her smile died somewhat. "Jacob, do you think we could keep this between us for a few days yet? I wish to tell my friends myself before they hear any gossip about it. I do not know how they will react to my upsetting their plans."

"If it means that much to you," Jacob said, "then yes. I can wait a while before we post the banns." And he needed to contact his family regarding the news. Should he do that before or after they married? After would be most prudent, he thought. His mother would want to make it into a big event; his father would likely try to run Claire off. The duke would not consider a governess to be a suitable bride for his spare heir.

How will she react to learning that she was to be a daughter-by-marriage to a duke? They hadn't spoken much regarding her opinion of the aristocracy, but he knew how much she valued honesty. Surely if she loved him, she would not mind. She would understand his reasons and forgive the deception.

But he did not wish to think about that right now. Jacob moved his head until there was only a whisper between their lips. "Now if you don't mind, I would like to focus on loving my bride."

"I thought you would never do so," was the last thing Claire said for quite some time.

CHAPTER EIGHT

"Children, I have some good news." Claire had entered the nursery after speaking with Mrs. Morrison. The children gladly left their lessons and clambered around her. "Your parents have written. They are arriving in a few days to host a house party."

"Brilliant," Peter and Michael cheered while Allison began to run in circles screaming. Sophie and Mary clapped their hands.

"What's more," Claire continued, gaining their attention again, "Miss Edwards, your mother writes that if you have been behaving, she will consider letting you take tea with the ladies one afternoon."

"Truly?" Sophie's eyes were wide. "She has written that?"

Claire nodded. "Masters Peter and Michael, your father is anticipating seeing how your horsemanship has developed. Miss Mary and Miss Allison, you are both to expect special treats from London."

"That's not fair," Peter complained. "They get treats and we just have to ride our horses."

"Master Peter, a gentleman does not begrudge his lot or the fortune of others," Jacob broke in from schoolroom door, where he was watching the scene. "Your father's message was somewhat vague; he may have more planned than simply watching how you ride."

"But—" Peter began.

"No buts." Jacob's tone was uncompromising. "Be grateful for all your father has provided you with so far; you could have much less than you do."

Peter bowed his head, chagrined. "Yes sir, Mr. Knightly."

Claire sent Jacob an amused smile. "Now, your parents will be interested in how you are progressing. Ladies, shall we go practice our music?"

Claire moved toward him on her way out of the nursery. "The Aldgates will be interested in your progress as well, Jacob. Be prepared to give detailed reports on the boys."

"That might be difficult," he replied in a low voice and a smile. "I've been spending all my waking hours thinking of you. Not to mention my nights."

Claire was sure her face had never been as red as she hurried after the girls toward the music room. Or felt as pleased.

Lucy entered the nursery with the tea tray, breathless and with a red face. The arrival of the lord and lady had sent the entire household in a frazzle. Claire had been proud of the children standing so still as they waited for their parents to descend from their coach. Only Allison, the youngest, had broken ranks to run to her mother.

"Cor, but the kitchen is hoppin' wit' all the foodies an'

nibbles to be made fer the party," Lucy complained. "Gets so a girl can't even make off wit' a proper tea tray."

Claire stepped away from Jacob, smiling at her friend. "We are grateful for anything tonight, Lucy. The children were so wound up with excitement they were difficult to settle in bed." She sat in the chair Jacob offered her as Lucy set down the tray.

"Well, ye best be pleased wit' what I brung you. Me light fingers even managed to lift this off Morrison's desk." Lucy brandished a periodical.

Claire gasped. "The London *Tattler?*"

"Brung by her ladyship herself ta read in the carriage. And now fer us," Lucy gloated.

"Don't tell me you read that rubbish," Jacob said, sipping his tea. But Claire was too engrossed in the gossip columns to notice his disdain.

"What it say, Miss?" Lucy asked, unable to read it herself beyond the simplest of words.

"There's a Lady H- who has retired to the country due to her delicate condition," Claire said. "Lords T-, A- and J- participated in a curricle race to Brighton that left Lord J- with a broken arm and several farmers with frightened cows that will no longer give milk. Lady S- and Lord C- were seen exiting the bushes in Hyde Park with twigs and leaves all over their clothes. Hmm, I wonder what they were doing," Claire added with a knowing smile.

Jacob wasn't listening. All the town gossip bored him, having seen and been a part of it for the last several years. He added a bit more whiskey from a flask to his tea and moved to stare out the window.

"Oh my," Claire breathed.

"What?" Lucy asked, her tone anxious and her face eager. Even Jacob glanced back at the two women hunched over the gossip rag.

"It says here," Claire read, "that the Earl of Rimmel has been missing for several weeks now."

Jacob froze. He had never presumed his disappearance from society would make it to the newspapers. Or that Claire would end up reading about it. He thought his family would have covered up the fact they had no idea where he was.

Claire continued reading. "He was last seen exiting the Duke of Maberly's townhouse in a state of extreme wroth. A source inside the house indicated that his father, the duke, has finally cut the Earl of Escapades off, refusing to pay any more of his debts or even a living allowance. This columnist suspects the earl to be hiding in the slums of Cheapside, the only place he can afford without paternal support. Debt collectors have been ringing the bell at the earl's bachelor lodgings endlessly to no avail; even his landlady claims she will not allow him back in without settling outstanding rent owed. Others have claimed not to even notice his disappearance aside from the fact that events are now more enjoyable without his presence to pollute the festivities. However, the length of the earl's absence is starting to worry some—perhaps something more disastrous has befallen the handsome peer?"

Silence reigned in the nursery. Jacob could not speak, could not even move. Would Claire put the clues together? His arrival at Aldgate Hall coincided with the date of disappearance. All his slip-ups—did she remember all of them? What would happen now? He risked a glance at her.

Claire put the gossip paper down. "What horrid things to say about a man. An earl, no less. To say they are better off without him? Those are people who have no respect. I have yet to meet anyone who is entirely worthless and would make life better by being absent."

Lucy patted her hand. "But ye ain't met much people of London, Miss. They be a different sort of people there."

Claire looked at Jacob. "Well, I have met two people from London that I hold in high esteem—Louisa and Mr. Knightly. And the Aldgates aren't all that bad—I certainly do not believe my life would be better off without any of them. No, I think the columnist has gone too far. Indeed, I pity the earl's family. They must be beside themselves with worry. I wonder if they have hired a Bow Street Runner?"

Not very likely, Jacob thought. His older brother perhaps would have, so long as he could keep it from the duke. But Jacob wasn't concerned about that. All he could do was look at Claire and wonder at how his love for her had grown exponentially in these last moments. Whatever happened in his life, he would never forget this moment, never forget the way she defended who she thought a complete stranger. Never forget that he did not deserve such a champion and likely never would.

Peter, Michael, and Allison all exclaimed over the horses while Sophie and Mary cooed over the fashionable dresses of the ladies descending from the coaches. All five faces were pressed against the nursery windows. From her place in the rocking chair, Claire smiled and answered the questions she could.

Jacob stood at a corner window, answering the questions directed at him, but largely keeping to himself. His attention on the arriving guests never wavered. He was intent on determining if he knew any of the guests, if any of them would be capable of unmasking him. So far none had seemed familiar. Such was the reason he had chosen to come to Aldgate Hall. He did not know Lord Aldgate himself, nor was he aware of any of his acquaintances knowing him either. It was a perfect place to hide. Until possibly now.

For a brief minute, he looked at Claire. She felt his gaze on her and looked his way, smiling the tender smile that she had taken to giving him. He returned her smile, wishing, not for the first time, that he really was simply Jacob Knightly, tutor. That man was worthy of her affection. That man was happy. That man had a future with the woman he loved.

Not so the Earl of Rimmel. Jacob turned his attention back to the coming coaches. The earl had little to speak of in regard to character. He could play a mean game of faro and *vight-et-un*, owned a set of prime goers for his phaeton, and had been lucky enough in a few investments. But he lacked substance, lacked character. As proven by that article.

Jacob pressed his forehead against the cool window and continued watching, continued wishing.

"I do not like it." Jacob's tone was mulish as he slouched against the wall of Claire's room, watching her ready herself in her finest dress. One thing he was looking forward to once this charade was over was providing her with dresses of the finest silk, muslin, and whatever other material she wanted.

Her best dress was at least three years old and only practiced eyes would be able to spot the repairs, but it still screamed of hardened circumstances.

Claire finished putting in her earrings and checked her hair again. "It happens all the time, Jacob. As Lady Aldgate said, one of the guests was delayed a few days by illness. I have evened out the numbers before." She looked at him through the mirror and smiled reassuringly.

"I wish I was going with you," Jacob said, frowning. "I would ensure your safety."

"I will be safe enough," Claire replied, pulling on her only pair of gloves. "The biggest risk is that I will be seated in the lowest seat next to a bore, which is what normally happens. And bores are nice gentlemen who just desire someone to listen to them, which I am capable of doing. I will be fine."

"There will be more than just bores seated at the table." Jacob had seen the young gentlemen as they had arrived. He recognized their ilk easily enough; he had been part of their ranks at one point. Those who thought servants, and especially governesses, fair game at any cost.

"I am under the protection of Lord Aldgate, Jacob. The guests will not wish to offend their host."

Jacob kept silent on that. He knew too many hosts who had been more than willing to turn a blind eye to behavior involving their servants. He captured her hand as Claire moved toward her door. "You will tell me if something happens?"

Her reassurance never wavered. "Nothing is going to happen."

"You will tell me." He squeezed her hand for emphasis.

"Yes, of course."

Jacob raised her hand to his lips and pressed a kiss on her palm. "I am looking forward to the day when I can buy you silk gloves. No more threadbare and worn fingertips for you."

Claire smiled and cupped his cheek. "I don't need things, Jacob, just you." She kissed him lightly on the lips.

"Enjoy your dinner, my lady." Jacob released her and watched her add an extra sway to her walk, just for him.

Jacob was not happy. He prowled the corridor above the library, cursing the Aldgates for not building a two-storied room with access from the upper hallway. If they had, he would be able to surreptitiously slip into the upper level to keep an eye on Claire instead of ducking into alcoves whenever footmen or Fosters were around the library.

Laughter emanated from the library, causing Jacob to frown. Four days now she had been called upon to even out the numbers in the evening entertainments. Her days, understandably, were dedicated to the children, but each night Lady Aldgate demanded Claire's presence, bemoaning the illness that had prevented her guest from arriving. Each night Claire assured him that nothing would happen—and nothing had. But Jacob couldn't escape the heavy feeling in his stomach that something was going to happen when he wasn't there to protect her.

He hated not being there to keep an eye on her. When they were married, when his deception was over, he would never let her out of his sight at house parties. Too many scandals and incidents occurred at such events; why the *ton* felt they were still suitable entertainments was beyond him. He knew what could happen at a house party for the basic fact that he had made a lot of those happen at the ones he attended in the past. No, being unescorted at a house party was not for Claire.

"Psst! Mr. Knightly!"

Jacob turned at the sound and saw Lucy sticking her head out of the servants' stairs. At her wild gesturing, he moved over closer to her.

"Ye can't be here no more," she warned him in a whisper. "Fosters has heard about it and ain't happy. He says yer spyin' on the guests. If he catches ye here—"

"I can't leave Claire alone in there," Jacob said.

"Ye must. Ye can't go in there yerself, so ye ain't doing nobody any good."

"But—"

"I'll ask William ta keep an eye on her," Lucy promised. "He's been in and out of there all night. He's first footman tonight on account of Ben bein' ill."

Jacob felt a modicum of relief. She wouldn't be entirely alone. With a nod of thanks to Lucy, he returned to the nursery to await Claire.

Claire stifled a yawn behind her hand.

"Never say we are boring you," a voice said at her elbow. She looked at Mr. Blatherly, a young man with puffy blond hair and kind brown eyes. He had been most solicitous to her since the first night, ensuring that she had partners for cards, charades, and the informal dancing. He did not appear to be so high in the instep that her position as a governess hindered his socializing with her.

Despite his kind attention, Claire often found herself wishing to be in the nursery with Jacob or he here with her. It made her uncomfortable to be parted from him for such a length of time. Since the house party began, they had barely any time alone together. Of course, Jacob came to her bed every night when she retired, but they didn't leave much time for talking. She missed hearing his voice.

She smiled politely at Mr. Blatherly. "Of course not, sir. It is merely my governess duties coupled with these recent late nights. I am unused to sleeping so little."

He smiled back. "That is a relief. Only we can find ourselves boring, whether it be real or practiced ennui. Heaven forbid someone not of the *ton* find us so. How lowering that would be to have the truth so pointed out to us."

Claire laughed. "Surely you are too hard on yourself."

"I disagree." Mr. Blatherly leaned closer to her on the sofa to whisper conspiratorially. "See Lady Tusset with her fan in the corner? I daresay she has naughty lines written on that fan just to keep herself from dying of boredom. And Lord Whittle looks about ready to expire if he has to hear one more fishing story from Lord Haggerty."

Claire looked at the people he pointed out. Sure enough, they were exactly as he described.

"But take Lord Percival and Lady Montgomery. See how bored they look with each other? I have it on good authority that when he visits her bedchamber tonight, both of them will be far from bored. One can even hear the sounds of their entertainment through the walls, or so I am told."

Claire stiffened and felt herself flush. "Sir, you overstep our acquaintance. This is inappropriate conversation."

Mr. Blatherly moved away from her. "My apologies, Miss Bannister. I forgot that governesses are the paragons of propriety that teach our children. It appears that mine failed to impart these important lessons upon me. Perhaps if she had looked more like you, I would have paid more attention."

Claire was saved from his awkward flirting by Lady Aldgate's beckoning. "Excuse me sir," she said and hurried over to her employer.

"I see you conversing with Mr. Blatherly, Miss Bannister." Lady Aldgate's tone held a hint of rebuke. "He is here courting Lady Tusset's eldest daughter. It would not do for you to think too highly of yourself."

Claire looked at the floor and nodded. "My apologies, my lady."

"It would be best for you to retire for the evening," Lady Aldgate said. "We no longer require your presence in the evenings. Lady Wroth has sent word, and we expect her arrival tomorrow."

"Very good, my lady. Thank you." Claire curtseyed and left the library, relief flooding her. She was glad to escape the guests. Even with those that showed her kindness, Claire felt judged by the peers. And found lacking. She longed for Jacob and hurried her steps to the nursery.

"Miss Bannister."

Claire automatically stopped and turned at the voice calling her. She rested her hand on the newel post. "Mr. Blatherly," she greeted, a little breathless.

He climbed the stairs toward her. "I did not mean to scare you away," he said with a smile.

She returned his smile politely. "Lady Aldgate no longer requires my presence."

"Ah. I am gratified it was nothing I did." Mr. Blatherly reached the top of the stairs and stood an appropriate distance away.

"Indeed not, sir. You were very kind and considerate to me." Claire bobbed him a small curtsey. "If you will excuse me, sir, I am retiring. The children rise early in the morning." She turned and started to make her way down the corridor.

She startled when she felt Mr. Blatherly's hand on her elbow. "Allow me to escort you to your room, Miss Bannister." He took her hand and tucked it underneath his, covering her hand with his.

Claire tried to pull her hand away, but he held onto to it tightly. "I do not think that would be appropriate, Mr. Blatherly."

He continued to smile at her. It wasn't threatening in any way, but Claire still felt uncomfortable. "It is always an honor to escort a lovely young woman, Miss Bannister."

She managed to tug her hand away. "I must insist, sir. I wish to retire alone."

His smile began to fade somewhat. "I have been nothing but solicitous. Surely I deserve some reward. Escorting you to your room is a small thing to ask."

"It is not small to me, sir, if I am to be honest with you. If it were found out, I could lose my position."

"It is just a governess position, Miss Bannister."

"To you perhaps, but it is my livelihood. A dismissal and poor character reference would ruin me."

Mr. Blatherly began to smile an all-too-different smile.

"You would be welcome to come to me for employment, my dear."

Claire raised her eyebrows at this. "I was unaware you had young children,. My congratulations."

He chuckled. "Nice try. But I am not in need of a governess."

Claire moved away from him toward the nursery stairs. "Then there is no position for me in your household."

Mr. Blatherly grabbed her elbow and turned her to face him, pressing her against the wall. "It wasn't my household I was thinking of, my dear. I would set you up in your own." He brushed some hair away from her face. "Surely you do not need me to spell this out for you. You are an intelligent woman." He stepped closer to her, pressing his pelvis into her belly, ensuring she knew exactly what his intentions were.

When his head began to lower toward hers, his lips puckered in an unmistakable form, Claire deliberately turned her head away from him. "I am betrothed, sir."

She heard and felt him smell her hair. "I can offer you more than a fumbling footman, my dear. A year with me will bring you more reward than a lifetime with him."

Claire's indignation was mounting. "Release me at once, sir, or I will scream."

A chuckle and a kiss to her neck. "And risk your position, the one you defended so thoroughly moments ago? Just a kiss, sweetheart, and I will let you go for the night."

"I will not betray my betrothed, sir." Her voice was firm and she pushed against his chest.

"Betrothal means so little in my world, marriage even less."

"Yet it is everything in mine," Claire replied.

"And in mine," a soft, dark voice said behind them.

Claire sagged against the wall in relief. *Jacob.* "Mr. Blatherly was just leaving, Jacob."

The man in question stepped away from her, releasing Claire from the wall. She moved away from him gratefully. Seeing Jacob standing in the nearby shadows calmed her nerves considerably.

"The fumbling footman, I presume," Blatherly drawled.

"I am no footman." Claire recognized the anger in Jacob's voice, even if Blatherly did not.

She placed a hand on Jacob's arm, hoping to soothe him. "Nothing happened."

His voice remained tight. "You and I have different definitions of 'nothing'." The sound of voices drifted up the stairs. Other guests were leaving the library. Jacob dropped a quick kiss on her temple. "Go to your room and wait for me."

Not wishing to provoke him further, Claire moved to the servants' stairs. The guests' voices were getting louder, and Claire had no wish to be caught in the corridor with two men.

"Say, do I know you from somewhere?" Blatherly asked Jacob.

"I highly doubt it." Jacob quickly racked his brain, but the man remained unfamiliar.

"I am pretty sure our paths have crossed. Are you a member of Brooks?"

"Do I look like I would belong to Brooks?" Jacob's tone was snide. White's was the family club.

"Mind your tone, Mr. Knightly," Lady Aldgate's voice called out down the hallway. Claire froze a merely two steps from the entrance to the servants' stairs. "Mr. Blatherly is the son of Baron Blatherly."

Still didn't ring a bell, thank God. "With all due respect, Lady Aldgate, I don't care if the man is first cousin to the king. He was molesting Miss Bannister."

Claire slid her eyes shut. She had hoped to still sneak away, escaping the notice of her employer.

The ladies' gasps echoed in the corridor. "Such language in the presence of your betters," Lady Aldgate trilled. "And accusing a peer of the realm? You will pay with your job, sirrah."

"I don't give a rat's as—"

"Jacob." Claire's quiet voice stopped him. "Please don't."

"Ah, the Jezebel," Lady Aldgate sneered. Jacob's jaw visibly tightened. Mr. Blatherly smirked. "I did warn you, girl."

"Warn her of what?" Lord Aldgate interrupted the scene. "What is going on here, wife?"

"I warned Miss Bannister not to set her sights on someone as high as Mr. Blatherly. Yet she was just seen in the man's arm. Accosting him, no doubt, in the hopes of bettering her station. Shameful."

Jacob glared at Lady Aldgate before turning to her husband. "It was Mr. Blatherly doing the molesting. I saw it."

"Are you sure we haven't met?" Blatherly persisted, looking at Jacob quite intently.

"Are you going to take the word of a tutor over that of our guest?" Lady Aldgate demanded of her husband.

Lord Aldgate released a long-suffering sigh. "I haven't done anything yet, wife." The last word was bitten out.

"Well, if Mr. Knightly is defending her, I am sure it is because he is in expectation of favors."

Claire's face reddened as the ladies twittered and giggled, pretending to be shocked. She hated this part of her job, the unfounded accusations merely because she was in service. As if that made her untrustworthy in and of itself.

"Mr. Blatherly," Lord Aldgate turned to the younger man. "What is your accounting of the situation?"

"I came upon Miss Bannister returning to the nursery," he said. "I saw her walking unsteadily and offered my escort. I know her to be tired, and likely she had imbibed more than she was used to—and on finer quality of spirits as well. Anything that may have happened has been misconstrued."

"That is a bald-faced lie," Jacob said, advancing on Blatherly. "I saw you pressing her against the wall and she was refusing your attentions." He stood nose to nose with the man.

"Mr. Knightly," Lord Aldgate warned. "That is enough. I cannot do anything when there are two contradicting accounts. Miss Bannister, return to the nursery. Mr. Blatherly, I apologize for this inconvenience, but please await me down in the library. Mr. Knightly, I will call for you later."

The group began to disperse, seeing the drama was over. Jacob stepped away from Blatherly reluctantly, fury still pounding in his veins. *To think this man had his hands on Claire.*

Blatherly's innocent face took on a smirk. "You're lucky I don't like an audience, otherwise you would have seen more than just her against the wall."

Jacob's right cross pounded against Blatherly's jaw, throwing him against the wall. He slid down to the floor with a stunned expression. Shrieks and shouts from the guests filled the hallway, and Lord Aldgate rushed to Blatherly's aid. Several of the women began to swoon.

Jacob turned on his heel and grabbed Claire's elbow. "Let's go, Claire," he growled, directing her to the nursery stairs.

"That's it," Blatherly croaked behind him. "You're the Earl of Rimmel."

Jacob froze.

Blatherly began to struggle to his feet. "What in bloody hell are you doing here? I thought you were missing."

"You are mistaken, Blatherly," Lord Aldgate said. "Mr. Knightly is our son's tutor."

"No, he is Rimmel, son of the Duke of Maberly," Blatherly insisted. "I may have been three years behind him at Eton, but I recognize him now. He was famous in the halls for his toasties and right cross."

Oh, bloody hell.

CHAPTER NINE

Jacob stared at himself in the mirror. The man in the reflection was one of the most familiar sights in his life, aside from longer hair than usual. Lord Aldgate had lent him the services of his valet and the use of a luxurious guest room for his transformation from Jacob Knightly, tutor, to the Earl of Rimmel. The clothes had needed some pressing, having been packed away at the bottom of his trunk, but now the man in the mirror sported a perfectly tailored bottle-green coat, pristine white cravat and collar, a cream-colored waistcoat, and brown pantaloons fitted tightly. Yes, it was a familiar sight.

Yet it no longer seemed right, seemed complete. The eyes were different. They still had the same confidence, the same basic self-assurance, yet there was something missing. The contentment was gone. And Jacob knew that it would not return, not without Claire.

Jacob sighed and turned away from the mirror, running his hand through his hair. She had disappeared when his identity had been revealed, and Jacob hadn't seen her since, her door locked and no response. Granted, he had been whisked away by Lord Aldgate, but her door had been guarded by Lucy upon his return; she had not been in the mood to help him. Not knowing what Claire was thinking or how she was reacting to the revelation was eating at him.

There was only one way to find out. Jacob had the morbid thought that he now could relate to men walking to the gallows.

It was odd, hearing the children's chatter coming from the nursery. Jacob had expected there to be silence, subdued talking at the most, not this laughter and high-pitched talking. It didn't seem right; it didn't reflect the burden his soul was carrying. He supposed this was one more lesson he was learning about how the world did not revolve around him.

Jacob swallowed and pushed open the door, interrupting the scene. Claire sat on the floor with the boys, close to the empty hearth, playing spillikins. From the looks of it, Peter was winning. Sophie and Allison were playing with the dollhouse while Mary sat on the casement bench with a book on her lap, unread as she stared out the window. Lucy sat on a chair in the corner, mending torn socks and pants.

Peter and Michael looked up at Jacob, and their jaws dropped. Scrambling to their feet, they rushed over to him. "Great Scott," Michael declared, "you look like a dandy."

"Nice watch," Peter commented, pulling out Jacob's pocket watch. "Where did you get it, Mr. Knightly?"

Claire spoke before Jacob had a chance to respond. She had risen after the boys and stood straight, spillikins piled up around her ankles. "Make your bows, boys, and girls, your curtseys. This is the Earl of Rimmel."

"Truly?" Peter asked.

Jacob cleared his throat. "Yes."

"You aren't a tutor?" Michael chimed in.

"Did Papa hire you to teach us about being gentlemen?" Peter questioned.

"Boys, your bows." Claire's voice was firm and uncompromising. With only a slight hesitation, Peter and Michael obeyed.

Jacob felt a tug on his coat. He looked down at Allison, the young girl gazing solemnly up at him. "I like your green coat. The buttons are shiny."

Jacob smiled. "Thank you." It was interesting experience, being complimented by a child.

"You honor us with your presence, my lord." Jacob looked at Claire, standing so straight, her voice so distant. Her voice held a tone that he had never heard from her before. "It is unusual to have guests outside of the family in the nursery." She gave him a slow curtsey, her eyes downcast as was proper.

Jacob swallowed. This was going to be difficult. "I was hoping we could speak. In private," he clarified.

"Lucy, could you please take the children outside? I believe there are some new flowers in bloom in the garden. When you come back, they can describe them to me."

Chaos abounded for several minutes as the children scattered to get ready. Jacob was called upon several times to offer opinions on appropriate clothing and toys to take along. Finally, the demons had left, and silence reigned in the nursery. Claire had not moved during the commotion; neither had Jacob. He stood staring at her for several long minutes. Claire kept her eyes downcast, but he could see the effects of a sleepless night around them.

"Claire," he began.

"The proper form of address for my position is 'Miss Bannister'," she said, adding a quiet, "my lord."

"Claire, please," he beseeched. "I'm still just Jacob."

"But you're not," she replied, at last lifting her eyes to his. The emptiness inside of them shocked him. "You are the Earl of Rimmel, son of the Duke of Maberly, and I am Miss Bannister, nobody."

He took a step toward her. "I may not be earl for much longer. I am the younger son. My brother's wife is due to give birth soon and if it is a boy, the title will pass to him."

"Semantics, my lord."

"Not really. When it comes down to it, I am still the same person."

"Yes, the same person who deceived an entire household into thinking you were someone you are not."

"I can explain."

"I am not sure I want to hear it."

"Please, Claire," Jacob said. "Just hear me out." He could see her mind working, different emotions flickering across her face.

"Very well," she finally said.

Jacob gestured toward the rocking chair. "Sit, please."

"I have agreed to listen to your explanations," Claire said. "I did not agree to bend proprieties."

"You do not have any hesitations in berating your betters," Jacob retorted, some of his frustration bubbling to the surface.

Claire stared at him, her eyes wide and empty. "I believe you, and I can agree that these are exceptional circumstances."

"Then please, sit," Jacob said again, "as these are exceptional circumstances."

Claire hesitated a moment before moving to the rocking chair. Settling her skirts around her ankles, she forced herself to sit straight. Her stomach pulsed with the need to pull her bedcovers over her head and hide from the world or, barring that, this man. In the hours since his deception had been revealed, she had felt all emotion leech out of her; she had given this man—this peer of the realm—her heart and her trust, and now it was clear that she was to get nothing in return, nothing back from this man. In retrospect, it was a risk she had voluntarily taken, but the result was the same: she was now empty, numb.

Claire raised her eyes to Jacob's. "I am ready to hear your explanation."

Pacing in front of her, Jacob ran his hand through his hair and took a deep breath. He had little idea where to start, in actuality. How could he present his situation in a manner that she would understand? Even more, in a manner that would achieve her forgiveness? He knew that he had violated her trust; he knew how highly she valued honesty. He knew that it would take much debasement on his part to regain her trust again.

Jacob pulled one of the smaller chairs to sit in front of Claire. He managed to get his large frame into it and clasped his hands in front of him, looking at her, hoping his sincerity was clear in his eyes. "Let me begin by saying how deeply sorry I am for hurting you. It was never my intention. You deserve more than that."

"Did you think no one would get hurt by this?" Claire

asked. "I am not even speaking of adults. You deliberately entered an environment with vulnerable, impressionable children. How do you think the children will react when you leave? How can you fully understand the extent of what you did? You are not the one who will have to cope with the results of your behavior."

"I know," Jacob said. "I know it now. Yes, I didn't think it through. But my time here has changed me. You have changed me."

"No, do not do that," Claire said. "Do not involve me in your scheme any more than you already have. I refuse to take any responsibility in this at all, not when I am the one you deceived the most. I gave you chances; I asked you about your life. I was entirely honest and expected to receive the same from you."

"Everything I told you about my life is true," Jacob defended. "I just omitted the fact of the title."

"But how I can determine beyond a shadow of a doubt that you are telling the truth now?" Claire asked. "You are looking at me the same way you have for the last weeks. I believed in your sincerity then, but now all I see is a stranger."

"Claire," he implored.

"I don't even know why you did it," she continued, rubbing her forehead. "Why on earth would you go to such elaborate lengths to disguise yourself? Whatever did you do to warrant even hiding your title? Is it something so scandalous and unpardonable that I shouldn't even ask?" She covered her mouth in horror. "Heavens, Jacob, did you get a young lady pregnant and refuse to marry her? Run from a duel? Kill a man in a duel?" The last words were strangled whispers.

"No," Jacob said. "No, I swear it, Claire. It is nothing so dire as that."

"Then why the deception?" Her eyes were full of sadness and confusion.

Jacob sat back awkwardly in the small chair, running his hand through his hair once more. He was sure Aldgate's valet would be dismayed to see his hard work destroyed so easily. "In retrospect, it was quite the foolish decision," Jacob began. "Knowing that merely increases my shame and remorse. As I said, everything I told you about my life, in particular regarding my relationship with my father, was true. I have spent my life in the shadow of my older brother. I learned early in my life that I could never live up to my father's expectations, so sometime during my time in Eton, I stopped trying. Instead of killing myself to meet the duke's high standards, I chose to live my life for myself, for my pleasure. Ironically, I received more attention from him once news of my escapades got back to him than I did while behaving properly, as a duke's son should. I started receiving monthly, if not more frequent, lectures from the duke on propriety and social expectations.

"Then Bradford married two years ago and now has a child on the way. I don't begrudge my brother the title, the marriage, or the happiness he has found; indeed, I am happy for him myself. But in my brother's successes, my father found more ways to demonstrate how I am lacking in every possible way."

Unable to sit any longer, Jacob pulled himself out of the chair and strode to the window. Leaning against it, he momentarily watched the children playing tag in the garden. So much for identifying flowers.

"It became harder to ignore his taunts and accusations. This past spring, after he had been presented with yet another gambling debt of mine, he said that I had to marry or be cut off. I refused, obviously, which precipitated a row like none we had before. During this, he accused me of being . . . nothing." Jacob swallowed the bitter lump in his throat before continuing. "He said that I was dependent upon his title and the title I carry, which was the result of nothing more than an accident of birth. He claimed that if I had neither, I would be found in a gutter after no more than a month, nameless and faceless. Going further, he said that I was a person society would not miss, as if I were a murderer or a thief."

Jacob turned back to face Claire, to gauge her reaction to his words. Her face was still, stony, her eyes on the chair where he had sat. "So I left. I told him I didn't need the title, didn't want it, that I could be a better person without it than he could be with his dukedom. It would be preferable to live poor but free than to live within the shadow of a courtesy title that I never asked for and be subject to a man such as him.

"I took nothing but the clothes on my back and the purse of coins in my pocket. Once I determined to be a tutor, I found clothing I thought to be appropriate to the position, exaggerated my way into an employment agency, and found myself on a horse cart on the way here a week later. You know the rest."

Claire continued to sit still, staring at the chair. She had heard every word he said, had absorbed every nuance of his voice, only to have it echo in the hollow regions of her heart. If he had told her this story a week, four days, three hours ago, she would have reached out in comfort.

Jacob moved back to sit in the chair, facing her. "In perfect honesty Claire, I was afraid that he was right, that I was worthless. Like a beaten dog, I began to suspect it was true and that I deserved everything he had ever said to me. I needed to do this to prove to myself otherwise; I needed to do this to regain my self-respect and pride."

Claire finally spoke. "It is a shame that in your quest for self-actualization you destroyed that of others."

Jacob reached forward and took her hands in his. "Claire, please believe me when I say I had no intention of hurting anyone. Especially you."

Claire gently tugged her hands away and stood; he automatically did the same. "Yet that was the result. As despicable as he sounds, it appears your father was correct about you. You once said that you tend to bring out the worst in people; you neglected to mention that you bring out the worst in yourself as well."

"You don't mean that," Jacob said softly.

"Perhaps not. Perhaps it is merely bitterness speaking," Claire said. She gave a small laugh. "Odd, since I am feeling no emotion whatsoever at this moment." She turned and moved toward her door. "Goodbye, my lord."

Jacob followed her. "Claire, wait." He managed to get to her door at the same time as she and held his hand against it, barring her from entering her room and shutting him out. "Surely what I did was not entirely unforgivable."

"What you did?" Claire repeated. "You believe that all you did was tell a lie. But it is more than that. I trusted you, yes, but even more, I trusted myself. And that is gone now, for I couldn't see you for what you were. That is what is unforgiveable."

"Only one of us is to remain here, my lord," Claire finished, staring at the doorknob. "As I am employed here and need to work for a living, it shall be me."

"Yes, I am aware of that. I will be in London for a few days, a fortnight at most, cleaning up this mess."

Claire gave a sad smile. She was now a mess. "Safe travels."

"I will return for you."

"I really wish you wouldn't, my lord." Claire brushed his hand off the door and opened it, slipping around him.

"But Claire," Jacob said, "I love you."

She looked him in the eye. "I don't believe you." She shut the door; all Jacob heard was the lock sliding into place.

Claire sat unobtrusively on a window seat, trying to blend in with the drapery. Lady Aldgate had invited her two eldest daughters down for tea for her visit with the minister's wife. The girls were behaving admirably, speaking when only spoken to and keeping their fidgeting to a minimum. As proud as she was of them, it freed her mind to wander. To think of Jacob.

She had never known it possible to dislike and miss a person so intensely and simultaneously. The depth of his betrayal had left her feeling shattered; had anything between them been honest and sincere, or had it all been a lie? Claire had spent the last few days sifting through everything he had said, everything he had done and she still failed to entirely determine what had been true and what had been falsehood.

How could she have trusted him so completely, so blindly? She had once considered herself a good judge of character;

now even her faith in herself was broken. She had given this man her heart, had welcomed him into her bed, had believed his proposal sincere, but it all meant nothing.

And he was a duke's son as well, from a world far above her own. His kind was the one she served; she was a member of the invisible class. From the start he had to have known that any relationship between them would have been impossible. Oh no, they had had the only kind of intimate relationship noblemen like him engaged in with women like her. What a fool she had been.

The worst was the nights. Despite her anger, her pain, her traitorous body ached for his touch. Missed the feel of his body alongside hers, yearned for the feel of his hands on her skin. Claire decided to add this to Jacob's list of betrayals: he had awakened her body to new sensations, only to leave her with no way to fulfill these new longings.

"Miss Bannister is going to have a baby."

Claire's head jerked up at Mary's voice, her eyes wide, her throat closed. Had she heard correctly? Judging from the sudden silence of the older ladies, they had heard the same thing.

"I beg your pardon, Mary?" Lady Aldgate asked.

"Miss Bannister is going to have a baby," the young girl dutifully repeated.

Claire half-rose from her seat at the window. "No, I—"

"I am sure you are mistaken, dear," Lady Aldgate said. "Miss Bannister would never do such a thing." She turned back to the minister's wife to resume their conversation.

"But I saw them," Mary insisted, unaware of the turmoil she was causing. Her need to be affirmed by her mother blinded her to all else. Her sister tried to shush her, but Mary would have none of it. "I saw her kiss Mr. Knightly."

Lady Aldgate wore a tight smile on her face. "Mary, this is not a topic appropriate for tea. Miss Bannister, take Mary to the nursery."

Claire hurried to do her bidding. Anything to remove herself from this situation. She would speak to Mary privately.

"No." Mary was growing louder the more distraught she became. "I saw it. I saw Miss Bannister kiss Mr. Knightly, and that's how babies are made. He was touching her bubbies and they were going like this." Mary opened her mouth and swirled her tongue around her lips.

Claire could only stand and stare, her hand at her throat. Both women were also staring at the young girl. In Mary's actions, Claire could see all of her hard work, all of her plans for her future, her reputation, slip away. Mary finally sensed that something was the matter. She slowly closed her mouth and gave Claire a wide-eyed, frightened look.

"Aren't you having a baby, Miss Bannister?" she whispered.

Swallowing, Claire forced herself to smile. She held out a hand. "Come, Miss Mary. We'll have a talk in the nursery, just you and I." Mary obeyed, crestfallen.

Claire was ready twenty minutes later when Lucy entered the nursery. "Beggin' yer pardon, Miss Bannister. Lord and Lady Aldgate are askin' to see ye in Lord Aldgate's study."

Taking a deep breath, Claire smoothed her skirts. "Thank you, Lucy."

"Erm, Miss Bannister?"

"Yes, Lucy?"

"It helps ta move yer feet. It's what makes ye walk."

Claire managed a tremulous smile. "Of course, Lucy, thank you."

Moments later, Claire could not even recollect walking to Lord Aldgate's study. It seemed as though she had just woken from a stupor to find herself standing in front of her employer's desk, his wife sitting on a nearby couch, staring stonily ahead. Claire absently noted that Lord Aldgate had not risen as she entered the room; Jacob always had.

"Ease yourself, Miss Bannister," Lord Aldgate said, not smiling. "You are not facing an executioner."

Claire did not answer, nor did she relax; she knew very well what she was facing.

"Right," Lord Aldgate began. "Lady Aldgate has informed me of what occurred in the drawing room."

"During a tea with the minister's wife," Lady Aldgate interrupted.

"She cannot be held responsible for your choice in guests, my dear," her husband chastised the outburst. Clearing his throat he continued. "Forgive me for this intrusion, but it must be asked: are you with child?"

The directness of his question took her by surprise, even though she should have been expecting it. As she struggled for a way to respond, he waved his hand in dismissal. "Allow me to rephrase. Miss Bannister, is there any credence to my daughter's allegations?"

Oh, how easy it would be to deny them, to dismiss Mary's words as childish imaginations. Very little would happen to the girl; the entire incident would be erased from people's minds, an inconsequential incident only to be remembered in whispers behind her back. Mary would heed the lesson well and only speak of appropriate matters. Claire would be able to remain at Aldgate Hall, continue teaching children of whom she was so fond, her reputation and future intact. The future of the Governess Club could thrive as well, their dreams still able to be realized.

But such behavior would be contrary to everything she had taught the children, everything she stood for. Mere days ago she had vehemently disparaged Jacob Knightly—his lordship, the Earl of Rimmel—for blatant falsehood; could she be so hypocritical? She was unaware if Mary had actually seen anything, but the possibility of her doing so was very real.

And if she denied the accusations and was later found to be with child? What would her employers think then? What would the children think of her; what would she think of herself? Mary had intended no harm but had acted as a young child desperate for her mother's attention and out of an urgent desire to be a participant in the conversation. No, Claire could not in good conscience lay this burden at Mary's feet.

Lord Aldgate was drumming his fingers on the blotter in front of him. Claire drew herself up and met his eyes, her gaze beseeching him to understand what she could not voice.

The drumming stopped; a noise of disgust escaped Lady Aldgate. "To think we had this—this—harlot around our children. I can only imagine what she has taught them."

"Hold your tongue," Lord Aldgate reprimanded his wife. "The condition of your presence during this conversation is that you are not to speak. You requested I deal with the situation; allow me to do so."

Claire did not fool herself for one moment that Lord Aldgate would advocate on her behalf. She had committed a grave sin and must be held to the consequences. The fact that she had been responsible for children when her erroneous behavior occurred merely increased the gravity of her actions.

Lord Aldgate sighed and rubbed his forehead. "It is shame that I have to do this, given your four years of service here. You will receive the wages owed you plus a fortnight more and a letter of reference. You are to be gone by morning."

"A letter of reference?" Lady Aldgate was indignant. "I will not—"

"You will provide a satisfactory reference," he told his wife in an uncompromising tone. "She has given us four years of exemplary service. I concede that she cannot remain here, but I will not be a party to ruining her life entirely. The reference need not be glowing, but must be satisfactory to her obtaining a new position. If you refuse, I will write one on her behalf, but you will feel my displeasure, wife."

Claire cast her eyes down and curtseyed. "Thank you for your generosity, my lord." With his nod of dismissal, Claire turned and left the room to prepare to leave yet another home.

She knew that she could not fully lay the blame on Jacob for this turn of events, but heavens, it felt good to.

Jacob stood at the sound of the door opening, his breath coming out in an anxious rush. It had been over a fortnight since he had seen Claire, and he was eager to lay eyes on her again.

His excitement was replaced quickly with disappointment

when he saw it was Lord Aldgate and not Claire. He masked his disappointment and nodded to the older man. "Aldgate."

"Rimmel." Lord Aldgate returned the nod and moved to the sideboard. He poured himself a drink without offering one to Jacob. "I must say I am unsure of the nature of your visit. Should I commend you for not skulking about this time?"

Jacob's jaw tightened, but he kept his voice even. "I am here to see Claire, Miss Bannister."

"Indeed? To what purpose?" Lord Aldgate settled into the chair behind his desk and gestured for Jacob to resume his.

"I fail to see how it is any of your business."

"You made it my business with your little escapade," Lord Aldgate. Jacob wasn't sure what infuriated him more, the man's presumption or his calm tone. "You involved my family and my children's governess; thus it is my business."

"Allow me to relieve you of the burden," Jacob said, his voice tight. "Bring Miss Bannister to the study."

Lord Aldgate examined his drink before taking a drink. "I cannot do that."

"I beg your pardon?"

"I cannot bring Miss Bannister to the study," Lord Aldgate repeated.

Jacob could feel a tic beginning in his cheek. "Yes, I heard you the first time. Care to explain why not?"

"I do not owe you any explanations, Rimmel, not after what you have done."

Jacob drew himself up. "You do realize who I am?"

Lord Aldgate looked him in the eye. "You are the man who brought deceit into my house and exposed my daughters to lewd behavior. You snuck in like a thief and stole innocence from this house."

Jacob was taken aback. "I beg your pardon?"

"It is quite annoying to hear you say that so often," Aldgate commented. "Do you really mean it? Or is it yet another lie?"

"Are you trying to provoke me?" Jacob asked. "I highly doubt you will enjoy the results if you are."

Aldgate sighed. "Rimmel, I do not have the time to sit here and trade threats with you; I do not even fully welcome you into my home. If you persist in your rashness, I will be obliged to act accordingly and," he looked Jacob in the eye again, his tone serious, "do not let my age fool you. I am fully capable of protecting what is mine. I do not need the protection of a ducal title to clean up my messes. Besides, your stunt has given me enough to not only embarrass your family, but to destroy someone you have shown to care deeply for. I have only prevented it thus far out of gratitude to her service here. Short of killing me, you have little to threaten me with."

Jacob ground his teeth together against the chill threatening to overtake his body. He had experience with embarrassing his family, but Claire? That was different. He would protect her at all costs. "All I wish is to see Claire."

Aldgate sat back in his chair. "That is impossible. Miss Bannister is no longer here."

"I beg—" Jacob stopped himself in time. "What happened? Where is she?"

"I do not know," Aldgate admitted after a moment. "She was dismissed from her post for her involvement with you."

"Her involvement with me? She told you?"

"Not quite. Apparently Mary had seen you two . . . being

intimate and brought it up to my wife. During tea with the minister's wife. I had no choice."

"But why wouldn't she wait for me or look for me?" Jacob was confused and couldn't stop it from showing.

"Is there a reason why she would?"

"She agreed to be my wife."

"Was that before or after your deception was revealed?"

Jacob hesitated for a moment. "Before."

"And you think that hasn't changed?"

"She did not say otherwise."

Aldgate gave a satisfied chuckle. "I am pleased to know that you will be held accountable to some degree for your actions."

"What do you mean?"

"Just that you have much to learn about women, son."

Jacob stared at the older man. "But she gave her word."

"One piece of friendly advice," Aldgate said, standing. Jacob automatically followed suit. Aldgate began to lead him to the door. "Women change their minds for the slightest of reasons, if any reason at all. How do you think a woman would react to being deceived in such a manner?"

"I need to find her," Jacob said. "Where did she go?"

"I do not know, nor did I care enough to ask. The moment she was dismissed was the moment she ceased to be my concern. She was a good governess, but still just a governess. Now get out of my house."

"If you would permit me one moment more of your time," Jacob asked at the open door. His horse was still saddled, waiting for him.

"What is it?" Aldgate asked impatiently.

A moment later he was on the floor, blinking at the ceiling that refused to focus. Aldgate gingerly touched his jaw; he would have a bruise like none he had received since his days at Cambridge. That Rimmel could pack a wallop.

Jacob mounted his horse and swung away from Aldgate Hall, not looking back. He knew of only one place Claire would go. If she wasn't there, well, he'd take care of that if it came up. All he could do now was pray that she was there and safe.

CHAPTER TEN

She couldn't believe it. Claire sat on her trunk and stared. She simply couldn't believe it.

Ridgestone stood where it had always been. Over five years had passed, and it appeared no one had lived in it at all. Neglect reeked from the grounds, the windows, the building itself. It looked not quite lifeless, but . . . dying.

Still, it was home. At least supposed to be home. Staring at it, Claire recognized the look of it, acknowledged the memories surrounded by it, but it did not resonate *home* as she had expected it would.

That could change. Would change. All she merely had to do was find a way to purchase it, write to the other members of the Governess Club, and with a little work, it would be home again. So what was stopping her? Wasn't this the start of the life the Governess Club had been discussing all these months?

Of course, the notice of new owners on the front door could be a hindrance. New owners were not likely to sell so soon, if at all.

Claire continued to sit on her trunk, staring at her child-hood home, unable to move. Unable to think.

A noise penetrated her fog. It started off quiet, but steadily grew, becoming more insistent. A horse. The rhythm of a slow canter was unmistakable. Blinking, Claire looked over her shoulder, stood, and turned to watch the horse and rider approach, her hands clasped in front of her.

She couldn't see the rider's face clearly, but she knew it was him. Knew it from the breadth of his shoulders, the length of his thighs, the hips that had been cradled between hers; her blood sang with recognition. The slight jump of her aware-ness both relieved and angered her; at least she could still feel.

Jacob reined in his horse and dismounted, watching Claire warily. She just stood there; was she even blinking? Or breathing? He couldn't tell. Lord, but she was beautiful. Weary and drawn, but breathtaking. Her beauty used to be quantifiable, but now she just was, without limitation. He moved toward her cautiously, drinking in the sight of her.

He stopped several feet away. "Claire," he greeted, inclin-ing his head but not taking his eyes off of her.

She curtseyed in return. "My lord."

Jacob smiled grimly at the reminder of their stations. "My sister-by-marriage recently gave birth to a son. I am no longer the Earl of Rimmel, just Mr. Knightly. I could claim a cour-tesy honorific but have chosen not to."

Claire did not speak for a moment. "Would you prefer my congratulations or condolences?"

"I would prefer your affection, if I am to be honest." He moved closer to her, but Claire stepped away. "I know you value honesty."

Claire gave a bitter laugh. "You know me well, do you?"

"Enough to know where you would come. To know that you have been disappointed too many times in life to forgive me easily."

"His Grace must be proud of your brother for gaining an heir."

"Yes, he is."

Claire couldn't stop herself from asking. "And where does that leave you?"

A corner of Jacob's mouth lifted in a roguish, yet hopeful smile. "Are you concerned for me?"

Claire sniffed. "Curious, at best. It would be nice to be ahead of the gossip columns for once." She ignored the fluttering in her stomach.

He acknowledged the hit with a tilt of his head. "Indeed. There is no need for concern on my behalf anyway. I am rich enough in my own right, although I am unsure of a particular investment I have made; the rewards are yet to be known."

Claire sat back down on her trunk and smoothed her skirts. "It fails to surprise me that you would make such a risky investment. Foolishness seems to be a trademark of yours."

"Perhaps." Jacob sat down beside her before she had a chance to object. "But I believe the rewards could be lifelong. I purchased an estate, you see, as a bridal gift."

Claire's heart seized; it was a long moment before she could breathe, let alone speak. "My congratulations are warranted after all."

"Thank you." His tone was mild and calm, a fact that she attributed to firing her outrage.

How dare he toy with her affections—cause her to fall in love with him and even welcome him into her bed—when he had an intended waiting for him in London? Oh, but he was more of a cad than she had realized.

Unable to stomach being so close to him, let alone his entire company, Claire stood and moved a considerable distance away from him. She kept her back to him, not trusting herself to remain in control if she were to face him.

Had any of it been true? Any of the words, kisses—did anything that had occurred between them have any sincerity at all? Or was she merely a diversion, a way to pass the time while he was in seclusion, pretending to be what he so clearly was not: a good, honest man.

Louisa was right; no man could be trusted. Each and every gentleman saw governesses as sport and at their disposal. Jacob Knightly was no different, even if he didn't have the title anymore. He had set out to deceive not only her, but everyone. And for what? A childish need to prove himself? Immaturity and selfishness oozed from his very pores.

"I am glad to find you here, actually," Jacob was saying. "I wasn't sure if I had missed you. I was prepared to keep searching of course, but that is no longer necessary, much to my relief."

"Heaven forbid I should be a bother to you." Claire could not keep the bitterness or anger from her voice.

"Following you would never be a bother, Claire," he replied softly. "I merely meant that I am relieved to find you safe and unharmed."

"Safe?" She turned to face him. "I suppose I am. But unharmed is another matter altogether."

Jacob lowered his gaze to the ground. "I know I have much to make amends for, and I do not expect you to forgive me easily. But," he said, lifting his eyes to hers, "I am prepared for the task."

"There is nothing for you to do." She wouldn't be around him long enough for anything he did to matter.

"I disagree. You can start by telling me how Ridgestone used to look."

Claire was startled. "Excuse me?"

Jacob rose and gestured toward the house. "Even I can see the neglect and misuse of the place. Tell me how it used to look; I will restore it to its former glory. And make suggested improvements, of course."

Claire could not believe her ears. He wanted to restore Ridgestone? "Wait—you are the new owner? You bought *Ridgestone* for your bride?"

"Didn't I make that clear?" Jacob asked, confused. Claire shook her head. "My apologies. After hearing you speak of it so much, I knew it was the perfect estate for me to buy. I wrote to my man of business several weeks ago and he negotiated the transaction. It helped that no one had purchased or rented it since your father; Lord Appleby was more than happy to part with it for a reasonable price."

Claire stared at him. Was there to be no end to his betrayal? She had trusted him, confided her dreams and plans for Ridgestone, and he had undercut everything by purchasing it behind her back. He knew the Governess Club wanted it; he knew what it meant to Claire to return here. And now to ask for her help in restoring it? Of course, it had to be liveable; she wouldn't argue with that. But to ask for her advice to prepare his future home with his intended? That was simply too much; new depths of his depravity and cruelty were being revealed to her by the moment.

Muttering furiously to herself, Claire marched to her trunk, picked up one end of it and began to pull it down the driveway. Her eyes burned with angry unshed tears. It would be a cold day in places unmentionable before she helped him prepare his bridal home. In fact, he should hear that.

"Claire, wait. Where are you going?"

"It will be cold day in H-E-L-L before I assist you in any way," she snapped at him.

"Claire, darling, what are you saying? What is wrong?" Jacob appeared in front of her and tried to grasp her shoulders. Claire shook him off, releasing her trunk in the process to fall on her foot.

"Ow," she howled, hopping on her good foot.

"Here," Jacob said, taking her arms and leading her to sit on her trunk. He bent down to examine her foot. "Are you in much pain?"

"Don't touch me," she said, shaking him off again. Her face was hot and wet with the tears she had been holding back.

Jacob released her and sat back on his heels. "Please tell me what is wrong."

She glared at him. "Need a list again, do you? Very well. What is wrong is that you stole my dreams. You stole my trust and my virginity. You stole my heart, Jacob. And everything you stole, you ground into ashes. I am nothing now, completely empty, because of what you have done to me. So please, go on with your life and your bride and leave me alone. I politely offer you the best wishes I can manage, but just leave me alone and let me find some way to become whole again."

Comprehension dawned on his face and he gave a rueful chuckle. "I suppose I've mucked things up again, haven't I. Once again I haven't made myself clear."

"Oh no, you've made yourself perfectly clear."

Before she could stop him, Jacob cupped her face and gave her a swift kiss. Claire reviled the part of her that ached for more.

"Oh, my silly governess. Too smart for your own good." He grinned at her. "You, my darling, are my bride." He dropped his hands to clasp hers.

Claire blinked. "What?"

"Did you really think I would buy Ridgestone for another woman? How callous do you think me?"

"But you said you had bought it as a bridal gift . . ."

"I have only ever asked one woman to marry me, Claire." His dear blue eyes were nervous. "I am hoping her answer has remained unchanged."

Claire bit her lip and glanced at the house, filled with memories and potential. She looked back at Jacob. "I don't know," she said honestly. "The hurt I feel, intentional or not, is so very real and deep. I don't know if I can trust you again. I don't know if I want to trust you again."

Jacob took a deep breath, hoping he'd be able to speak before the despair closed his throat. "I suppose I deserve that."

Claire cupped his cheek. "I can't say I don't agree with you, but I am sorry."

He pressed a soft kiss to her palm. "What can I do to change your mind?"

"I don't think there's anything you can do except give me time. Time away from you," she clarified. "I need to think and having you near will likely just confuse me more."

Jacob's head dropped and nodded slowly. "I understand," he said in a strangled voice.

"This may be a good thing for you too," Claire said, trying to make the situation better. "You may find someone else and—"

"There will be no one else," he said, looking at her. "No one but you, Claire."

"You must be realistic."

"I am." Jacob pushed himself to his feet. "One good thing about being a simple mister is the lack of expectations on me. There is no need for me to worry about someday holding some lofty title; God forbid anything should happen to my family to make that come true. But it does mean that I can choose my own bride, my own love, and give her the time she needs. I will need to learn to be a patient man, but I will have no other woman as my wife if I cannot have you."

Claire was taken aback by his impassioned words. "Oh."

He reached into his coat pocket and withdrew a paper. "This is for you."

She took it, a questioning look on her face. "It is the deed to Ridgestone," she said, reading it. "My name is on it."

"I did say I bought it for my bride," Jacob reminded her.

Claire swallowed and held it out to him. "I am not your bride. Not yet."

"By rights Ridgestone should be yours. Take it, I insist."

"I will not be beholden to you in any way," Claire said. "I wish for no complications in our situation."

"Then buy it from me," Jacob suggested. "I will have my man of business draft terms for payment."

Claire nodded. She could accept that. "But they must reasonable, not overly generous. I do not want to feel I owe you anything."

"Agreed." Jacob helped her stand and shook her hand, businesslike. "Now if you will allow me, I recently acquired the skill of carrying luggage. I can carry your trunk inside for you."

"Thank you." Claire followed behind as he unlocked the front door and brought her trunk upstairs to her old room. She had thought that her first steps upon her return would be filled with delight and wonder at seeing her old home again, but she could not take her eyes off the man in her room.

Jacob bowed to her, desperately wanting to take her in his arms and kiss her breathless. "Adieu, Miss Bannister." He turned and left her bedroom, wanting to get the moment of departure over and done with.

"Wait," Claire called out from the stairs as he reached the front door. He turned back, hope flaring in his chest. "How will I contact you if I—when I have an answer for you?"

Jacob swallowed. "I will return in three months. If you have not come to a decision at that point, we will discuss matters then. For everything else, you may contact my man of business. To reduce the complications."

Claire nodded. "Thank you."

He bowed again and was out the door. As the sound of his riding away, all Claire could think about was how quiet Ridgestone was. How empty.

Jacob stood at the drawing room window gazing out, his hands clasped behind him. Before his eyes, an unkempt lawn was slowly turning brown, and leaves were beginning to sparkle with the orange and yellows of autumn. His eyes recognized this but did not process it; they were focused on finding something—someone—in particular.

He could not deny the charm of Ridgestone. After nearly three months of inhabitancy, the Governess Club had shaken off the shadows and chills the previous neglect had wrought, bringing light and life back to the old building. Seeing it now as it was, Jacob could imagine it as it had been during Claire's childhood, and he did not begrudge her attachment to the place. If the frugal elegance of the drawing room was any indication, the members of the Club had done well.

Jacob turned away from the window to stand against the mantle. Mismatched figurines decorated various sections of the mantle, broken up by small portraits and landscapes drawn by obviously amateur hands; a large oval mirror with burnished gilt edges hung on the wall above, affording those facing the fireplace a view of the entry. A small set of fire pokers stood securely to one side of the empty hearth.

The colors were not what Jacob had expected of a drawing room that belonged to a household of ladies. Instead of lacy frills of pink and white, the colors were muted, but welcoming. Blue was the dominant theme, a lighter shade on the walls and darker navy for the furniture; white trim and friezes accented nicely. Taking a seat on one of the long sofas, Jacob was again surprised to find it comfortable and able to support a man of his physical stature. Nudging a small wicker basket beside the sofa, Jacob found an assortment of rag dolls, tin soldiers, wooden animals, and books. Clearly, younger children were welcome in this room. Perhaps that was the purpose of the darker-colored furniture, to minimize the visual damage of mishaps.

Jacob stood as the door opened to reveal a winsome blonde. Dressed in modest pink muslin, she smiled at him as she approached. "Thank God you have finally arrived," she said breathlessly, her eyes twinkling.

"I beg your pardon?"

"Do you not remember me? I am Miss Louisa Hurst."

Jacob automatically bowed. " Miss Hurst. I am Mr. Jacob Knightly."

"I know," she replied, her eyes still twinkling. "I remember you from the assembly."

Recognition dawned on him. "You are one of Cla—Miss Bannister's friends."

"And you are the one who broke her heart. Has anyone offered you tea?"

Jacob found it difficult to reconcile the welcoming face with the directness of her words. "No, thank you. I am fine. I am here to see Miss Bannister."

"Of course you are; I am not an idiot, sir. Please sit." Louisa took a chair, arranging her skirts as Jacob resumed his seat.

"Is she not here?" He hadn't considered the possibility. Of course, he was a few days early from the three months he had promised, but he had been unable to stay away much longer.

"She is teaching," Louisa replied. "She has been informed a visitor is waiting for her, but we do not stop lessons except for emergencies. We are private tutors for hire, and, as such, our clients expect to get what they paid for."

Relief followed quickly by anticipation flooded his veins. Thank God she was here. Just knowing that she was in the same building as he made his nerves leap. "Of course. I would not expect it otherwise. How have you found being here at Ridgestone, my lady?"

She smiled; Jacob was momentarily stunned by its effect. What was this beautiful young lady doing making her way as a private tutor, and as a governess before that? Obviously her situation had been reduced much as Claire's had, but why hadn't any man stepped up to marry this beauty? And why had her father or brother allowed her to take on such a role in life? They ought to be ashamed of themselves.

"It has been a godsend," Louisa said to his question. "All of us are so content here. We are able to choose whom we teach and when, and even what we teach. Claire teaches the arts, Miss Sara Collins the sciences, and I teach languages."

The small talk was killing him, but Jacob forced himself to be interested. "Indeed? Which languages are those?"

"The usual for young ladies: French and Italian. I also know rudimentary Latin and Greek, so am able to begin that education with the young boys."

"Impressive. Forgive me, but I thought there were four members of the Governess Club?"

"Bonnie has yet to join us."

The voice from the doorway had Jacob leaping to his feet. Claire stood there, staring at him, her green eyes wide. How had she entered the room without him noticing? All the breath and blood in his body seized at the sight of her. The urge to gather her in his arms and kiss her breathless nearly overwhelmed him.

Claire couldn't stop staring at Jacob. When Louisa had asked her to meet with a guest in the drawing room after her lesson had finished, she had assumed it was to greet a potential client. They had only been accepting clients for two months, but their reputation as educators had already begun to grow. The nearby villagers may still be wary of single young ladies living independently, but they could not discredit the quality of tutoring their children received.

Instead it was Jacob. Here. In her drawing room. Where her mother had taught her to serve tea. She had sat for countless hours in the room, stitching, embroidering, learning how to be hostess, asking her mother for advice, entertaining guests, and later mourning both parents. But nothing had prepared her for the sight of Jacob Knightly standing in this room.

Heavens above, but she had underestimated the effect seeing him again would have on her. He had been dangerous as a simple tutor, but now, dressed in town finery? This Jacob Knightly was ruthless; just from looking at him she could feel her breasts tighten and her body soften. The tan pantaloons that hugged his thighs disappeared into gleaming black Hessians. Ivory white linen surrounded his throat, tied in a simple but perfect knot. The brown coat was so finely tailored it seemed as though it had been sewn onto his shoulders. Even his hair, long and unkempt as a tutor, had been precisely cut into a fashionable array.

Despite her physical and emotional response to his arrival, everything about this Jacob Knightly just emphasized how she didn't belong in his world.

Jacob bowed to her. "Miss Bannister."

Claire curtseyed. "Mr. Knightly."

They stared at each other. "You look well," Jacob said. "Are you?"

"Yes, I am. And you?"

"Yes, thank you."

They stared at each other. "How is your nephew?" Claire asked.

Jacob smiled. "A credit to his father and mother. Doesn't stop howling, though."

Another moment passed. "I didn't expect you for five more days," Claire said.

"I am sorry if I have inconvenienced you. Would you prefer I return later?"

"No, no, that is not necessary."

"Oh for heaven's sake," Louisa said. "Claire, stop this nonsense and show Mr. Knightly the garden."

Coloring, Claire gestured to the door. "Would you care to see the garden, Mr. Knightly?"

"Thank you, I would." Jacob offered her his arm and was gratified that she took it after only a momentary hesitation. He could not explain why he was acting this way; he had never felt so tongue-tied or nervous in his life. Even when he had first proposed to her, his usual confidence had been beneath the surface. But now? She held his heart and his happiness in her hands. What would she do with it? His palms began to sweat.

Claire shivered as they stepped outside. "Are you chilly?" Jacob noticed and asked. "Would you like me to fetch your shawl?"

"No, I am fine. I will adjust in a moment. I enjoy the freshness of autumn."

Jacob admired how tanned her skin had become. "You have been spending time out of doors."

"Yes. I have taken charge of the garden area." She gestured around them. "We haven't yet tackled the lawn, but I've been tilling and planting seeds in this area. Most of the flowers will not bloom until spring, but I am enjoying the sight of the tilled soil. There is an inherent promise to it."

"I am looking forward to showing you the gardens at Maberly, the ducal estate. My mother takes an active role in cultivating them as well and is justifiably quite proud. I have mentioned you to her, and she is eager to meet you."

Claire fell silent at the mention of his family. Jacob swallowed; this was not a good sign. He began to harden to heart by degrees.

She gestured toward some trees. "I am hoping to eventually put in a wilderness walk through those trees. It would assist Sara in her science lessons. She enjoyed the story of how you taught Peter and Michael potential and kinetic energy."

"For the love of God, Claire," Jacob said, pulling her to a stop. "Put me out my misery. Do you have an answer for me, or do you need more time?"

Claire stared at his chest; she clenched her hands against the memories of caressing its breadth vibrating through her fingers. Snapping her mind away from such thoughts, she said, "I have an answer for you." Her voice was soft.

Jacob stepped away from her and turned his back to compose himself. All indications of her refusal were written on her face, her posture, her very essence. Turning back to her, he said, "I will say now before you give your answer that if it is a negative one, I will not give up. I will continue to pursue you. Telling me no will not rid you of me."

Her eyebrows arched. "Are you intending to bully me into submission? Is that your idea of a marriage proposal?"

"It is an unfortunate reality that one cannot live without one's heart. As you possess mine, I have no choice but to remain in your life. I love you, Claire; I will not give up on you, on us."

"It cannot work," she said.

"I disagree."

"We have always disagreed on matters of importance."

"Then defend your position. Why can it not work? Give me one of those lists you are so fond of."

"Very well, but it is you who is fond of lists," Claire replied. "Firstly, there is the Governess Club. We have just established ourselves here and are gaining a reputation. I will not jeopardize all of our efforts."

"I see no reason why they cannot continue here at Ridgestone," Jacob said, taking a step toward her. He needed to be close to her, close enough to kiss. "That point is moot."

Claire narrowed her eyes and took a step away. "Secondly, there is no guarantee you will remain so generous. You will have influence over the fate of our endeavor."

"How so?" A step closer.

A step away. "Upon marriage, all of my property will revert to my husband. You will once again be the legal owner of Ridgestone and will have the authority to evict my friends."

"Another moot point," Jacob replied. "I have already had

my man of business draft a marriage settlement that leaves Ridgestone in your name."

Claire blinked. "Excuse me?"

"I have no wish or desire to own Ridgestone. I will live here with you, but you will be the legal owner. It was your dream to be here as its mistress and owner; I will not take that from you." A step closer.

"Oh." Claire was flummoxed. She hastily took a step away. "But I haven't finished paying you for it."

Jacob shrugged and took a step toward her. "Then keep paying me."

"That doesn't make sense. My money would be your money, so in essence, I wouldn't be paying you at all." A step away.

"Every payment you make I will put into a trust for our daughters so none of them will find themselves in a situation like yours." A step closer. "While we will never live in the first stare of fashion or comfort, I am wealthy enough to modestly support a wife and family."

A step away and Claire felt a tree at her back. She swallowed. "Our daughters? Have you no wish for sons then?"

Jacob stepped closer once more and braced himself with one arm above her head, cupping her cheek with his free hand. "I wish for healthy children with you, male or female. I will be the most fortunate man alive if I had you, sons, and daughters, but believe me when I say what I wish most for is you. I will not disappoint or fail you or our children in the way your father disappointed and failed you."

"My father didn't disappoint or fail me," she whispered.

He ran a thumb over her cheekbone. "Yes he did, my darling. I cannot fully condemn him, as it brought us together, but you should not have gone through what you did. I dedicate my life to your happiness and security."

"Still, it cannot work," she said.

"Why not?"

"Because you are a duke's son," Claire burst out. "Just look at the difference in how we are dressed. You were raised in riches and greatness; I was raised in this. You are a duke's son and I am the daughter of a country squire, a nobody."

Jacob swallowed. "You are the woman I love, the woman I will have as my wife. These things you mention? They are meaningless. All I am wearing are clothes; they are nothing. Would it make you see reason if I weren't wearing them?" He pulled away and shrugged off his coat.

"What are you doing?" Claire asked as he pulled off his cravat and began to unbutton his waistcoat.

"Showing you that underneath these clothes, I am just a man. You are just a woman and I am just a man, Claire." The waistcoat joined the other clothing on the ground. "These things are frivolous trappings. Yes, life is easier with them, but they are not necessary."

"Jacob, stop," she said as he began to tug his shirt out of his pants. Claire's eyes darted around them, and she placed a hand on his chest to prevent him from removing it. "Someone might see." Heavens, her fingers tingled from the heat of his skin through the linen; the hard muscles pounded with the rhythm of his heart. Claire licked her suddenly dry lips, imagining the taste of his skin on her tongue.

He gathered her hand in his, pressing a kiss to her knuckles. "I am just a man, Claire, nothing more, nothing less."

"But what will you do here?"

Jacob shrugged. "Whatever I want. Whatever you want. I can manage the estate so you can be freed to teach. I can teach our children to manage estates and other skills that may be necessary in their lives. I could be your dancing master. I could help Miss Hurst teach Latin and Greek. But mostly I could be your husband, your partner. I could be yours, Claire."

Claire looked into his eyes. "Could we actually do this?"

"Do you love me?" Jacob's face was serious.

She nodded. "So very much."

"Then yes, I believe we can. Or at least," he added with a playful smile, "we could certainly have some fun trying."

Claire laughed. "Then ask me again."

Jacob bent one knee and looked up at her. "Miss Claire Bannister, will you take me as your husband, for richer or poorer, in sickness and health, lacking a title, no matter what clothing I am wearing or not, and despite my birth, over which I had no control?"

Claire nodded. "I will."

"Praise be," Jacob said. He stood and gathered her in his arms and finally, finally kissed her breathless.

Want more of the Governess Club?
Here's a sneak peek at part two:

BONNIE'S STORY

An Excerpt from

THE GOVERNESS CLUB: BONNIE

My dearest Claire,

Felicitations on your betrothal to Mr. Knightly. I am simply overjoyed for you, for there is no one more deserving of happiness than you. Does he by any chance have an unmarried brother you can mention me to? I am almost too embarrassed to admit how much I giggled at my pitiful joke. We are in much need of levity at Darrowgate these days.

I sincerely wish that I could be with you during the planning of your wedding. I simply cannot justify leaving my charges at this time. The upheaval that would be caused by my departure, so soon after the tragedy that claimed their parents, would devastate them. Henry walks around for all appearances an old man with the weight of the world on his shoulders; a younger, more solemn viscount I have not seen. And Arthur—poor Arthur. He continues to cling to me; we have not heard him utter a sound since that day and his thumb sucking returned shortly after the funeral.

There is more, however, and I can feel my cheeks heat with indignant anger just thinking about it. I have oft heard the term "fair-weather friend" but had yet to experience it. Indeed, I feel ashamed to be placed in the same category as these people, as I am sure you, Sara, and Louisa will as well.

The servants have been abandoning Darrowgate— abandoning Henry and Arthur, if I am to be blunt. The guardian chosen in the late Viscount Darrow's will has yet to arrive and Mr. Renard refuses to release any money to pay wages on the grounds that it exceeds his authority. Exceeds his authority, indeed! For more years that I have been a governess here, the man of business has always paid out the servants' wages. Several of the maids here send money home to their families; I know the stable master has a wife and three young mouths to feed, and he is only one of many in such a situation. Exceeds his authority, indeed! Yes, I know I am repeating myself, but it bears so. That is clearly a sign of how distraught this situation has made me.

With this in mind, can I truly blame the servants for leaving an uncertain prospect? Part of me does. Have they no loyalty to Henry or Arthur? Or to the viscountcy? Most have been here longer than I and yet they have fled at the first sign of trouble. How can a boy of eight years be expected to manage a household? I am not sure which angers me more: their disloyalty to the viscountcy or their callous abandonment of two young children entirely unprepared for life as orphans. Has honor and integrity disappeared amongst the servant class?

I must be completely honest with you, dearest Claire; even from this distance I can feel your steady gaze on me, silently asking me questions and patiently waiting for me to answer. Your concerns are not unfounded. I have not fully recovered from the incident either. There are times when I wake in the middle of the night hearing the screams of the horses mix with those of Viscount and Viscountess Darrow. Have you ever noticed how similar the sounds of screaming humans and horses are? And at times the memory of the coach mangling before me is so real I fear I could touch it. Even now, the sound of a coach approaching paralyzes me. I refuse to force the boys to ride in one, but I wonder if that is more for my sake than theirs.

Of course I am aware that recovery is likely to quicker away from Darrowgate, but I refuse to abandon Henry and Arthur in their present condition, even if I were not suffering my present abhorrence of coaches. Remaining here until the guardian arrives will be best for everyone, I believe. Hopefully the wait will not be much longer; it has already been over a month since the accident.

Please convey my regrets to Louisa and Sara for not being able to fulfill my part of the Governess Club at this time, but as I described, present circumstances are not ideal. I do beg you, however, please do not mention my own struggles. I would not wish any of you to concern yourself with this. There is much to occupy yourselves with your wedding and establishing our club's reputation. I will recover; it is only a matter of time.

I miss all of you, my dear friends and sisters.

  With all my love,

  Bonnie

ABOUT THE AUTHOR

Ellie Macdonald has held several jobs beginning with the letter t: taxi-driver, telemarketer, and most recently, teacher. She is thankful her interests have shifted to writing instead of taxidermy or tornado chasing. Having traveled to five different continents, she has swum with elephants, scuba dived coral mazes, visited a leper colony, and climbed waterfalls and windmills, but her favorite place remains Regency England. She currently lives in Ontario, Canada. The Governess Club series is her first published work.

Visit www.AuthorTracker.com for exclusive information on your favorite HarperCollins authors.

Give in to your impulses . . .
Read on for a sneak peek at four brand-new
e-book original tales of romance
from Avon Books.
Available now wherever e-books are sold.

SKIES OF GOLD
THE ETHER CHRONICLES
By Zoë Archer

CRAVE
A BILLIONAIRE BACHELORS CLUB NOVEL
By Monica Murphy

CAN'T HELP FALLING IN LOVE
By Cheryl Harper

THINGS GOOD GIRLS DON'T DO
By Codi Gary

An Excerpt from

SKIES OF GOLD
The Ether Chronicles
by Zoë Archer

The Ether Chronicles continue when
Kalindi MacNeil retreats to a desolate, deserted
island after surviving the devastating enemy
airship attack that obliterated Liverpool. Kali soon
discovers she's not alone. Captain Fletcher Adams,
an elite man/machine hybrid—a Man O' War—
crashed his airship into the deserted island, never
expecting to survive the wreck. But survive he did.

Her heart climbed into her throat. Edging along the gravel-covered base of the hills, she moved slowly onward, telling herself stories of goddesses who'd braved hordes of demons without fear.

Yet she was no goddess. Only a woman, completely on her own.

A shape appeared out of the mists. A large, dark shape. Heading right toward her. It moved noiselessly over the gravel in spite of its size.

She grabbed her revolver, aiming it at the shadow.

It immediately stopped moving. Then it spoke.

"You're not from the Admiralty."

A man. With a deep, rasping voice. As if he hadn't spoken in a long time.

Even through the heavy mist, she saw that he didn't hold up his hands, despite the gun trained on him.

"No," she answered, her mouth dry. "Not the Admiralty." Yet she didn't want to tell him where she *was* from. She had no idea who this stranger was.

"Anyone with you?" he demanded. He spoke with an air of command, as though used to obedience.

Despite the authority in his voice, she kept silent. Telling him she was alone could endanger her. At least she was armed.

He didn't seem to care about the revolver in her hand. He moved closer, emerging from the fog.

Oh, God. He was big. Well over six feet tall, with shoulders as wide as ironclads. His body seemed a collection of hard muscles, knitted together to make the world's most imposing man. He had black hair, longish and wild, as if he hadn't seen a barber in some time, and a thick beard, also in need of trimming. He stood too far away for her to see his eyes, but she could feel his gaze on her, dark and piercing, hyper-vigilant, like a feral animal's.

And he stepped still nearer to her.

"My father was in the army," she said, her voice clipped. She raised her gun. "He was a crack shot. He trained me to be one, too. Stay where you are."

She thought a corner of his mouth edged up in a smile, but the beard hid his expression. "I'd knock that Webley out of your hand before you could pull the trigger."

Words poised on her lips that no man could move that quickly—he was still ten feet away—but those words faded the more she looked at him. His massive hands could likely crush a welder's gas tanks. But more than the raw strength he exuded, a palpable but unseen energy radiated from him, something barely contained.

She couldn't tell whether she was fascinated or terrified. Or both.

"You're doing a poor job of putting me at ease," she answered.

Again, that hint of a smile. "Never said I wanted to put you at ease."

"Not another step," she snapped. Instinctively, she moved back, out of striking distance. But as she did, her left boot caught in the rocks, and she stumbled.

Unseated, the stones tumbled down in a small rockslide. They knocked her down, twisting her leg at an unnatural angle. She sprawled on the ground.

Instantly, the stranger darted forward, a frown of concern between his brows.

She kept the gun pointed at him, despite lying awkwardly upon the rocks. "Back. I'm fine."

"Your leg—"

Her skirts had come up, revealing both her limbs.

The stranger must have been civilized at one point, because he quickly turned his gaze away.

"Go ahead and look," she said. "I gave up on modesty months ago."

He did, and when he saw her leg, he cursed softly. "Mechanical."

An Excerpt from

CRAVE

A Billionaire Bachelors Club Novel

by Monica Murphy

New York Times and *USA Today* bestselling
author Monica Murphy launches her sexy
Billionaire Bachelors Club series with
the story of Archer and Ivy: a lavish bet,
a night of carnal desires, and a forever
they never thought possible . . .

Ivy

"**W**hat is this?" I take the wadded-up fabric from his hand, our fingers accidentally brushing, and heat rushes through me at first contact.

"One of my T-shirts." He shrugs those broad shoulders, which are still encased in fine white cotton. "I knew you didn't have anything to wear to . . . bed. Thought I could offer you this."

His eyes darken at the word "bed," and my knees wobble. Good Lord, what this man is doing to me is so completely foreign that I'm not quite sure how to react.

"Um, thanks. I appreciate it." The T-shirt is soft, the fabric thin, as if it's been worn plenty of times, and I have the sudden urge to hold it to my nose and inhale. See if I can somehow smell his scent lingering in the fabric.

The man is clearly turning me into a freak of epic proportions.

"You're welcome." He leans his tall body against the doorframe, looking sleepy and rumpled and way too sexy for words. I want to grab his hand and yank him into my room.

Wait, no I don't. That's a bad, terrible idea.

Liar.

"Is that all then?" I ask, because we don't need to be standing here having this conversation. First, my brother could find us and start in again on what a mistake we are. Second, I'm growing increasingly uncomfortable with the fact that I'm completely naked beneath the robe. Third, I'm still contemplating shedding the robe and showing Archer just how naked I am.

"Yeah. Guess so." His voice is rough, and he pushes away from the doorframe. "Well. Good night."

"Good night," I whisper, but I don't shut the door. I don't move.

Neither does he.

"Ivy…" His voice trails off, and he clears his throat, looking uncomfortable. Which is hot. Oh my God, everything he does is hot, and I decide to give in to my impulses because screw it.

I want him.

Archer

Like an idiot, I can't come up with anything to say. It's like my throat is clogged, and I can hardly force a sound out, what with Ivy standing before me, her long, wavy dark hair tumbling past her shoulders, her slender body engulfed in the thick white robe I keep for guests. The very same type of robe we provide at Hush.

But then she does something so surprising, so amazingly awesome that I'm momentarily dumbfounded by the sight.

Her slender hands go for the belt of the robe, and she undoes it quickly, the fabric parting, revealing bare skin. Completely bare skin.

Holy shit. She's naked. And she just dumped the robe onto the ground, and she's standing motionless in front of me. Again, I must stress, naked.

My mouth drops open, a rough sound coming from low in my throat. Damn, she's gorgeous. All long legs and curvy waist and hips and full breasts topped with pretty pink nipples. I'm completely entranced for a long, agonizing moment. All I can do is gape at her.

"Well, are you just going to stand there and wait for my brother to come back out and find us like this, or are you going to come inside my room?"

An Excerpt from

CAN'T HELP FALLING IN LOVE

by Cheryl Harper

Cheryl Harper returns with another fun, fresh tale
from the wacky Elvis-themed Rock'n'Rolla Hotel.
Summer's hit Memphis, and things between Tony
and Randa are about to heat up. She's hiding
something, and he's determined to make her
come clean. She may be up to Tony's challenge,
but can Randa handle the fire between them?

He pointed at the pool. "Show me what you can do, Miss Captain of the High School Swim Team." Gorgeous pools and cloudless days like this one weren't meant to be wasted, not even by expensive girls who lived in fear of wrinkles.

Randa started to shake her head but changed her mind. He could see the second she decided which face she was going to put on. She ran a teasing finger down his arm, and he fought a shiver. "You've got it, Tony."

She stood beside the lounger and reached up to peel the floppy straw hat off before she shook out her hair. Tony hoped he wouldn't be required to contribute to the conversation. Anything that came out of his mouth this second would sound like, "God, yes. Please, yes. Show me the suit now."

Randa dropped her sunglasses on the hat and slowly unbuttoned the white, long-sleeved, gauzy cover-up before stripping out of it quickly. She let it drop from her fingers—

right onto his lap—and Tony nearly nodded his thanks. His eyes were glued to her. He'd hoped for a bikini. Those hopes were dashed. Instead she wore a pretty conservative one piece that was cut high on the hips and low enough to tease at the V of her breasts. And the rest of her was nothing but perfect, satiny skin. "Still too skinny, Tony?"

He nodded and tore his eyes away from her hips, her tiny waist, and her perfectly sized breasts to watch her face.

Her teasing smile slipped a bit, and he thought he saw honest desire in her eyes. She took an awkward step away from him and then seemed to remember her audience. She turned and glanced over her shoulder before moving to stand at the end of the pool. She executed a flawless shallow dive and made four quick trips up and down the length of the water. He tried to be objective. She was a clean, fast swimmer. But none of that mattered. She could be doggy-paddling and refusing to get her hair wet, and he'd still think she looked amazing. He watched her float around aimlessly for a minute or two before she swam over to the side of the pool.

The sight of her climbing out was unforgettable. Possibly life changing. More than anything he wanted to kiss her, strip her, and take her. With her hair wet and slicked back from her face, he could see teasing, intelligent blue eyes. And her body would bring stronger men than Tony to their knees. It was a damn good thing the sight of a water drop disappearing into the shadow between her breasts had frozen his tongue and nailed his feet to the concrete. He might have embarrassed himself then and there.

Instead he nodded mutely as she slipped into her cover-up and asked, "Meet you in the lobby at four?" He watched her move quickly across the hot concrete in her bare feet and felt the despair of a man who was going shoe-shopping soon.

He didn't want her to burn her feet. Or to be unhappy. Or to be here for anything other than to see the finest Elvis-themed hotel in the world. He wanted her to be a normal girl, maybe one who worked nearby. One he could have met at the bookstore.

He watched Randa pause at the door to the hotel and scan her room key. Before she disappeared inside, she smiled and waved at him over her shoulder. And he and his frozen tongue loosened up enough to say, "Shit." He was in for it. No matter how this turned out, he was going to have regrets. She was here through the weekend. That was enough time to fall under her spell and give up all the hotel's secrets. That would be just about right. From famine to feast to famine again so quick he'd probably lose his mind.

Then again, if he didn't go any further with her, he'd spend unhealthy amounts of time thinking about her wet and half dressed. Probably for the next fifty years. She was like the world's most perfect steak. He couldn't let her go, but eating her would ruin other steak for him.

Eating her? Apparently the brain breakdown had already set in. He shook his head as he grabbed his towel and went to his apartment.

An Excerpt from

THINGS GOOD GIRLS DON'T DO

by Codi Gary

Katie Conners is finished being Rock Canyon's good girl, and, after one too many mojitos, she starts making a list of things a girl like her would never do. When the sexy local tattoo artist finds Katie's list and offers to help her check off a few of the naughtier items, Katie may just wind up breaking the most important rule of all: Good girls *don't* fall in love with bad boys.

She tried to pull away from him, cursing the tingles his warm hand caused. Glaring, she attempted to sound firm, "Let go of me. I'm tired of your games. I don't know why you think it's funny to play with someone's emotions, but I've never done anything to you, and I find it humiliating that you would make fun of me over something I did when I was having a bad day. It makes you a bully, and I want you to leave me alone."

Chase didn't release her, just reached out with his other hand and started to pull her toward him. Her heart pounded as all that mouthwatering muscle drew closer to her and he slipped his arm around her waist. *She* might think Chase was lower than pond scum, but her hormones sure didn't agree.

Katie stopped struggling and tilted her face up just as he said, "I can't do that."

She froze as he let her wrist go and trailed his hand up her arm slowly, making every single cell in her body scream to get closer but a lifetime of good breeding and manners kept reciting: *Good girls don't . . . good girls don't . . .*

Still, the part of her that hadn't been held by a man in a long time wished we would kiss her until her brain shut up.

He didn't kiss her like she wanted him to, though.

Chase ran one hand through her hair and cupped her cheek with the other. "Sweet Katie, the last thing on this earth I'd want to do is upset you, but I have to say, it is really hot to see you all riled up." He slipped his thumb over her bottom lip and continued, "Your mouth purses when someone irritates you and you're trying not to say anything. I've noticed you do that a lot. But your eyes heat up when you're ticked off, and that's hard to miss. Like now."

Katie was holding her breath as she swayed toward him, and he whispered, "Do you know what you want?"

Did she? "Yes." She drifted a little closer, unable to resist him. It was his eyes. No, the way he smiled. Maybe . . .

"Do you know where you want it?"

His words were penetrating the fog of desire, and she blinked at him. "What?"

Sliding his hand from her lip to her shoulder, he asked, "Do you want it here?"

She finally registered what he was asking and said, "I don't want a tattoo."

"Are you sure?" he said teasingly. " 'Cause I have a binder full of things you might like. Of course there are some items we could check off the list that don't involve binders, needles, or tattoos. Let me think . . ."

She needed to move away from him so *she* could think. She took a breath, but that was a mistake. He smelled amazing, and she was so tired of being good all the time. She was thirty years old, and the man she was supposed to spend the rest of her life with had picked someone else. Maybe if she had been more daring and less rigid, Jimmy wouldn't have dumped her. She would never know now. She couldn't change the past, but she could let go now, just this once.

Slipping her arms up around his neck and ignoring his surprised look, she said, "Chase, if you want to kiss me, will you just do it already?"